What You Can't Give Me

also by R.C. Binstock:

The Light of Home
Tree of Heaven
The Soldier
Swift River
Native Child
The Vanished

What You Can't Give Me

Incidents from an Unexpected Era

R.C. Binstock

cover painting by Katarzyna Maciak

R.C. Binstock Books
copyright R.C. Binstock, 2022
all rights reserved

ISBN: 9798353520788

Kindle Direct Publishing, North Charleston, SC

for the dead and the living
the sick and the healthy
the jobless and the waged
the homeless and the housed
the brave and the fearful
the endangered and the safe

and in memoriam
John Robert Seybold, 1945-2022
a true and beautiful friend

Contents

Year Zero

..

You know I'd give you everything I've got for a little peace of mind
I'd give you everything I've got for a little peace of mind
I'd give you everything I've got for a little peace of mind

— "I'm So Tired", Lennon & McCartney, 1968

Where the Heart Is

She surprises herself by hoping, fiercely, when Troy walks into the office and picks up the phone, the ringing phone two feet away that she has been desperately trying to will herself to answer yet another time, that whatever the caller says will make him smile. It's a totally preposterous hope, sure, but it's all she's got.

He glances at her—OK, he's clearly concerned, she has to pull herself together a little, she's the *boss*—as he puts the receiver to his ear. "Morgan and Morgan," he says, with impressive anticipatory sympathy, "how can I help you?"

The other party is talking and Troy is definitely not smiling. "Oh, no," he says. He glances at her again and *she* manages to smile, a little.

"Okay, Raffy. It's okay. Let's hope that's the worst for today. Yeah, okay. Don't worry. I don't know what he's doing but he'll be on his way soon as he can. Just take twenty and relax, you need a chance to get over something like that. Or maybe if you can find someone in worse shape than you, help them out."

He puts the receiver in the cradle, very gently, and sighs. "What is it?" she asks.

"He's getting two at Metro and one of them is over three-fifty. They ran out of pouches so they had him in a regular bag and there was no one to help, so Raffy of course tried anyway and it ripped."

"Fucking shit."

"His phone is discharged and he's so upset the only number he could remember was this one. I'm going to find out what Rocco's doing—"

"He's trying to get the fucking permits filed but the system's totally wedged, it's taking forever. Then he has to get Areg Katourian. The man's wife has been calling every hour to say 'He's still here, please come get him.' Petrov just cleared it—after only nine fucking hours. She called us at six this morning, for god's sake."

He puts his hands on his hips as she rants, which looks quite fussy until she realizes he is restraining himself.

"With all respect, Sarah, you might want to take a look at your language. I get it, but I'm afraid you'll slip and say the wrong thing to the wrong person."

"Okay, yes, thank you."

"Also, worth bearing in mind that Petrov and whoever did that to Raffy and all the others are dealing with the same conditions we are. And they're all mad at someone too."

"Do you really have to keep making so much sense?"

"Assuming you can handle the office—"

"*Yes*," she says.

"—I'll finish the permits, and if Mrs. Katourian has been waiting with her husband for—" he glances at the wall clock "—ten and a half hours it doesn't matter if it's another two. I'll talk to her, alright?"

She slowly stands up. "Sure. Fine. I'll go tell Rocco while you call her."

"You okay?"

2

"No. No, I'm not. I didn't know I was signing up for this, Troy."

"None of us did."

It's not like she's inexperienced. Young to be in charge, maybe, a little young, but she grew up in it. She knows what she's doing, knows the business. It happens sometimes, that people for one reason or another find themselves in a situation that is somewhat unexpected. And then a major emergency involving, well, everyone comes along and ends up going well past unexpected, all the way through crisis to out on the wire with no net. Which means experience is for shit; you just have to cope.

Things will slow down eventually. She knows that. It's very hard to have faith in it, though, when she's working on two hours of sleep and someone from a family that's been on the books for twenty years comes in angry. Things have gotten so serious, so quickly.

Yesterday it occurred to her that this has become a sort of circle of life thing, except with the focus on a particular spot on the circle. *Our spot.* Her father would like that. She can hear him saying, "Life gives way to death, death to life." She is not sure if he actually said that or she made it up but doesn't care.

Her father would be angry too. Way beyond angry. He would be appalled if he were here. One thing she knows for certain he would say: "It's a disgrace." But he would rise to it. So what choice does she have?

Before the end of the day tomorrow she will have to repetitively state, several times, possibly many times, the already widely publicized fact that there are no funerals to be had, that they are not *allowed*, the best she can maybe offer, if by any chance the cemetery in question has not yet banned visitors altogether, is to

3

ask them to pause so clergy can say a few words to a *very limited* number of immediate family members before their loved one is interred. Five minutes, tops. And they will hate her for it. She will have to explain to several more families, again in all likelihood repeating it multiple times to each, that not only are the crematories closed to visitors but their own deceased's cremation will be delayed, deplorably delayed, because facilities across the county, the state in fact, are maxed out, and see that look in their eyes as they try to grasp that what they are about to go through—spending every minute of every day thinking about their mother or husband or daughter lying alone somewhere and not knowing how much longer—is happening to *that many other people* at the same time. Which most will not find the least bit comforting. And they will hate her too. She will have to listen again to Annie's lecture—every afternoon like clockwork, exactly two and three-quarters hours into her three-hour stay—about how she has taken on so many jobs for people who can't pay and may never be able to that the business will crater in six months, tops. And she will hate Annie for it even as she appreciates it, even though Annie is right, because neither Annie nor anyone else has explained to her what the fuck else she can do.

She actually laughed, when he asked her. Then she saw the look on his face.

"Sorry, Pop, that was disrespectful. But didn't we talk about this? Like a couple years ago?"

"Things change," he said more quietly than he almost ever said anything.

"I'm still feeling pretty much the same about it."

"We don't have a lot of time." Not quite looking at her.

"How do you mean?"

"I mean I don't."

And now she's up to her neck in chaos. Because of him. And strangely, even though she wants to scream, she isn't sorry.

In the morning she is slightly calmer. Just very slightly, but still. Troy arrives and (also like clockwork) she feels the inevitable wave of gratitude for his presence. He's been around, literally, despite his relative youth, having worked homes from Portland to Charlottesville, and has an astonishing store of knowledge and good judgement; it's like he's held onto every little thing he ever watched or was told. Compared to him she's still an apprentice. He's also steady, thoughtful, funny, and attentive, and even if he were not any of those there is no fucking way she could get the place through this without him.

No spoken greeting, but his smile is enough. Truth be told it's perfect for the job; totally sincere, projecting good will, not in the least suggesting there is anything right with the world.

"I talked to Maritza," he tells her, in a get-ready-for-bad-news tone, after stashing his worn but sturdy backpack under the table.

"What'd she say?"

"One case."

"*One*?" It's hard not to panic. They have to use this stuff, it's prescribed by the state, although she knows of no way it's different from any other disinfectant.

"She said we're getting that much because she likes me."

"What the fuck do we do?"

"Language."

"*Sorry*. Whatever will we do?"

"I'll keep working on her."

"Yeah, well, that's the thing Troy, they all like you, who can blame them, but maybe you should like them back more. If you know what I'm saying." Trying to joke is idiotic, but *one case* hit hard and she is suddenly back to pushing off despair for another half hour.

"Have you seen Maritza?"

"She's not so bad."

"Not my type."

"And who is?" Which she instantly regrets because he'll give her that look, the look for which there could be multiple explanations if she were up to reviewing them, though just one is at all likely.

But it's only a sigh this time. "I know you're being worn down by this like the rest of us," he says. "I promise I'll find more before we need it." As he goes through the door she thinks *do I look that tired?*

That she liked the work so much was a big surprise at first. But it came to her over time that labeling it duty to her father was one of those silly self-delusions. She wouldn't have taken it on if she hadn't, well, wanted to. Although she'd always known it was important, it wasn't long before she appreciated that from a more mature perspective, and the gratitude touched her deeply. But now it's important in a different way. Before, her father was like some sort of priest; now his daughter's the drudge pulling a wagon through the village, that gets heavier as she goes.

She can't honestly say for sure that in the six years he's been gone there hasn't been a morning she's come in and passed some remainder of him—his portrait opposite the front door, the candelabra they picked out together not long before he went into hospice, his hat still on the office coat stand—without thinking of that moment, of the pause that seemed endless before she threw herself into his arms. But there haven't been many.

She can hear him advising her, every day. Counseling patience. Taking the long view. Reminding her that no matter how much she cares or how closely she pays attention she cannot share the grief of the bereaved, just respect and support it. That these circumstances, however bizarre and stressful, don't change anything for them—they're still people who've lost a loved one, the way it's always been and will be.

She can also hear him saying, "Call Cornell. He loved me. He loves *you*. You can do this on your own, sure, but why would you want to try?"

They stand looking at the bodies, lying tightly packed together in a space not intended for them.

"Someone has to go. We have four there and Troy said they're getting impatient."

"We don't have anywhere to put them."

"You still have to go."

"Where will we put them?"

"That's why I'm leasing the cold truck."

"If it ever gets here."

She just looks at him.

"Soon's I get back they'll have another one for us."

"Raphael," she says. She is very, very tired. "Please. Go pick those people up. Saint Joe's has much bigger problems and they're stacking them to the ceiling. Apologize to Jillian and Doc Santiago if he's around and get them and bring them back, okay? Don't argue with me."

She is not too tired to see that he is now silently weeping. She puts her hand on his arm.

"It all of us, Raffy. Everyone is slammed. Kresge and McAllister. Rosen. I guarantee you there is someone at every one

7

of those homes, every home within fifty miles, who wants to go and collect remains as little as you do. Plus it's the hospitals and the crematories, the diggers, it's the same for everybody dealing with this. Do you want to be the one who breaks down? Who can't hold on a little longer?"

"No."

"Then get the van and go."

After sitting at her desk for a couple of hours, trying to get organized while simultaneously taking rapid-fire calls—that's exactly right, the goddamn phone might as well be a machine gun—she goes to the loading dock for air. It's quiet now, but both the van and the hearse are due back with more bodies any minute, a dismaying prospect given their existing inventory. Which calls to mind last week's warning from Joey the equipment guy (whom she suspects of regularly bumping her to the top of his queue, which must have been very long in this case, because he'd like to date her). "We're on a whole other level of hard already and it'll get much worse," he observed as he buttoned up the hydraulic lift. "I don't think any of us remotely knows how hard it'll get." After pausing so she could absorb that he added, "But I don't have to tell you, it was always a tough line to be in and it still will be when this is over." While she doesn't know what "tough" means to Joey, she has to agree: there are things that will never get easier, not when this lunacy has ended, not if she runs the home for another fifty years.

Being around grief all the time, for example, really all the time, one way or another; yeah, it is punishing, if anyone is wondering. And you don't get used to it unless you're a jerk, the kind who's always laughing at the job no matter what. But the worst part is when you suddenly find yourself resenting them for it, like, *get the fuck over it already*, and feel like dogshit on the sidewalk.

Then there's routinely having to deal with close family members—two or three siblings, a parent and their kids, husband and wife—who have seriously divergent ideas about who the departed was and what they wanted, not just for a service but in life, and according to them never got. It's like wildly conflicting gossip that in the absence of the subject you could never straighten out. And you have to dance around it every time you're with them until the job is done because if it breaks out into the open they'll never forgive you; in the case of a full ride, viewing hours and wake and procession and so on, that can be a lot of dancing.

Maybe the worst, though, is timing. Which matters because unlike most jobs, it's always personal. If someone has never been called on to provide comfort and direction to a numb, continually weeping, or manic but destined to crash survivor three times in the middle of the same night, and that immediately after having a major blowout with their Aunt Mary, she doesn't know how she would describe it to them. Except to say that it pisses you off on behalf of all concerned. Still you have to be a pro, everyone's counting on you. You can't snap at a mourner and then say, "I'm so sorry, I've had an upsetting couple of days." You have to produce the comfort and direction and nothing but the comfort and direction. She imagines most performers of all types would recognize her inescapable moment, when she stops by the mirror in the foyer to tell herself *It doesn't matter what just happened or how you feel. You're on.*

Rocco sorely wishes he could take it back. Like everyone else he's slowly losing it and the last thing he needs is to be trapped in the van with Sarah after she got a flat and couldn't wait for AAA to come (which they aren't going to do at all, not being morons) because she had a vicious backlog when she left the office (against her better judgement) to make a "curbside pickup" (that could have waited) and knew by the time she was pounding her steering wheel and screaming curses at the bastard who left the nail in the street that it had already doubled.

"My father? You never knew my father." She is tapping a pen on the dashboard. She never does stuff like this and finds it annoying in others. But she's been tapping the pen since he picked her up. She's become the character in a bad movie who's like a bomb about to blow.

"I've heard enough about him—"

"Oh you have, have you? Well next time you see him, ask him why the *fuck* he got me into this *fucking nightmare*, huh?"

"He didn't—"

"He didn't love me like he thought he did. Wouldn't you say?"

It was a first date, sixth or eight months before the roof fell in. The guy was not bad looking and far from stupid, and he knew what she did and seemed not to mind. They were having fun, talking and laughing about first date things like music and movies, travel experiences, dumb friends they had when she paused to catch up on her dinner. After a few seconds she glanced up to find him studying her. *Or maybe,* she thought, *just liking what he sees.*

"Is it lonely?"

"I'm sorry?"

"Correct me if I'm wrong, but while your work is utterly necessary and appreciated in the moment, I'm sure, it's not exactly on anyone's top ten list. Is it?"

She wanted to say, shut the fuck up and eat. But why ruin the evening?

"We're all on our own, honestly," she managed after a few seconds. "We're all whistling in the dark. Don't you think?"

This one would be horrible any time it happened. It is not made any more horrible by the intolerable context because it's already as horrible as it could be. Her high school friend Mona's mother died abruptly and to everyone's shock of COVID-19, getting Mona halfway to *maxime horribilem*, as they would have said back in Latin II, and then her father shot himself before the sun rose again with a handgun she didn't even know he had.

In a way Sarah is impressed that Mona is even on her feet. There is not remotely enough room beside this latest horrible for the only slightly less recent: Mona's split from her husband, the guy everyone went nuts over when she took him around the neighborhood one Christmas, because (as several classmates told it) she caught him in bed with his personal trainer, who laughed at her—presumably he found it funny she didn't know her husband liked men—and supposedly temporary move into her parents' fairly small place right before the lockdown hit and she lost her job. She has horribles stacked up like planes waiting to land.

"How could he think of it, Sarah?" Mona asked when she called. The ringing had pulled her from a sleep so deep she needed a minute to fully place the caller and grasp what she was saying. Mona was not crying then and is not crying now. She is just thoroughly, determinedly, vigorously angry. Which makes a lot of sense really. But the difficult thing is she is focusing it all on her father, giving a pass for the moment to the virus, the doctor who said it was too early to bring her mother to the hospital, her husband, the trainer, her brother in California who she doubts she will ever even hear from again, the owner of the catering company who the instant she realized what they were looking at cut all her employees loose without so much as a week's wages, and anger that broad and deep squeezed into a spotlight on one deceased man is very intense indeed. As both a friend and the funeral director of record (*who will never*, she can hear Annie foretelling, *be paid*) she faces a major challenge: she absolutely can't join in, she can't so much as momentarily begin to look like she is possibly considering *defending* him, she can't just nod silently. She has to keep coming up with something to say that reflects her appreciation of the horribleness and her eagerness to help without suggesting for a moment that there is anything that might make it less horrible.

They are sitting in the now unused viewing room, a good eight feet apart, over coffee Raffy actually brewed for them, Mona (who has decided to aggressively not care about infection risk) masked only because Sarah told her (fibbing only a little) that if anyone from the city saw unmasked people in the home they could be shut down. *Even you, Dad*, she thinks, *would be up the creek on this one.* She can't for the life of her remember his ever having said a word about handling a suicide, but maybe that's because it wouldn't have done her any good.

"How could he think of making it so much worse for us?" asks Mona. It has taken a while to figure out, but Sarah is now sure that the "us" she keeps referring to in her ceaseless variations on this question is herself and her mother's corpse, which was of course still lying in their bed when he did it and is of course lying there now. "How could he even think of leaving us alone long enough to load the fucking thing?"

"I can't begin to imagine," she answers, trying to thread the unthreadable, "because I can't begin to imagine his state of mind after your mother—"

"What about *my* state of mind? Pretty fucking horrific, I bet you can imagine *that*, but I didn't leave *him* alone."

Troy knocks on the doorframe and comes a step or two into the room. *Oh, thank god.*

"Ms. Lambrusco," he says without preamble, "I'm sorry to intrude, but Ms. Morgan described your situation to me. Your indescribable situation. And I had to tell you how sorry I am, and that if there is anything at all I can do to help you through this painful time—and I do mean anything at all—I urge you to tell me what it is."

He is working his magic, all right—when Mona says "Thank you, appreciate that" it is the first time since she called that she has sounded anything other than furious—but Sarah is slightly alarmed because this little speech, while worthy of several of her oilier peers, is not really Troy. She glances at him and as their eyes meet grows more alarmed than that.

"We see so many extremely painful situations, Ms. Lambrusco, and as you can imagine we don't compare or rank them. It's just a great deal of human pain and we simply do our best to support and comfort those who are bearing it. So when a situation"— there's that word again, it's not a Troy word—"stands out, when it is strikingly tragic, well, our hearts truly go out to those whom it has befallen."

"Mona, this is Troy Jenkins. He's been working with me since July."

"I won't say it's nice to meet you, Mr. Jenkins," says Mona. Sarah has to admit that his audience is responding well to his delivery, much as she loathes it herself. "But you're right that it's striking. Stricken is exactly what I feel. Struck over the head. By my own father."

"That must be an exceptionally painful way to feel," says Troy, sounding at last as if he is pushing himself rather than sliding smoothly along. "I can only share my observation that in my experience, Ms. Lambrusco, those under the impact of sudden, shocking grief are often entirely unaware of the impact of their actions."

"Oh, he was *aware*," answers Mona, shaking her head. "I'm absolutely certain he was *aware*."

"I know," he tells her, a pained tone creeping in, "that it can be terribly, terribly hard when a loved one—"

"*Loved one*? Not anymore."

She has never seen Troy look remotely like this. He is glowering at Mona. That's the only word for it. No effect for a couple of seconds because his target has closed her eyes. But then he says it aloud.

"Really? I mean, *honestly*?"

They are both riveted. He has just broken one of the funerary prime directives: never, ever, *ever* question *anything* said by the bereaved. Mona may not know she understands what he's done, but clearly she does. Sarah feels as if she is again 13 and watching her dog get hit by a bus.

She quickly rises. "Mona," she says, doing everything she can to regain her friend's attention, "you and I are going to be waiting for some time, and I think it will do us both good to walk around a block or two."

"Mr. Jenkins," she says, turning quickly to Troy before Mona can say a word, "I haven't had the chance to tell you that Mr. Fiore badly needs your assistance with that paperwork we discussed. Badly. Will you go back there and help him, please? *Right away*?" As she speaks she takes a step or two toward him and is astonished to smell alcohol. Well, "astonished" doesn't begin to cover it.

"Yes ma'am," he replies, and turns to leave. Back still to Mona, she says quietly but very, very intensely, "*No more fucking liquor, Troy.*" Watching him disappear, gathering her strength, it comes to her in a moment that while it's absolutely clear he should be fired immediately, she doesn't want to do that. It's not that she has mixed feelings; she doesn't want to at all. She's not even offended or upset.

"Mona," she says, gesturing her through the door toward the foyer, "I have to be brutally honest. I'm beyond impressed, stunned actually, that you can do *any* of this. Given what you must be feeling. Conversing with me, contacting family, making decisions. I always knew you to be strong, but this is something else altogether."

She hears shouting in the background. *As bad there as here.* And now she's adding to his troubles.

"What do you think I should do, Cornell?"

"What do *I* think you should do? Who cares what I think?"

If anything could amuse her right now, that would be it.

"I do. My father came to me in a dream—well, nightmare, really, if you know what I'm saying—and said 'Call Cornell.'"

"Want to make sure I have this straight. You're asking me for advice about something entirely personal?"

"Not at all, C. He *works* for me. Without him I wouldn't last a week. Which I know should absolutely not be a factor in our relationship, and vice versa. But it *is*. It would be even without all this terrible shit, and here I am making decisions that may be bad for my business on account of that relationship. But if you think I can keep spending eighteen hours a day not doing enough, letting everybody down—which if you're wondering I do realize is also what the rest of you are going through—without knowing he'll be here to help, you have a highly unrealistic view of my capabilities. And by the fucking way, why would I not ask you something personal?"

15

"Do you like him? Never mind, I can tell you do."

She stifles herself and waits.

"You never heard of mom and pop?"

"What the hell is that?"

"Married couple running a business together. Used to be common as dirt. Lunchroom, dry cleaner, candy store et cetera."

"You mean like 'Sarie 'n Troy's Main Street Mortuary, Since 2020'?"

"Something like that."

"We're not a couple. So far it's just that he wants to be. And Dad passed the business to *me*."

"Oh for Christ's sake, little girl, *work it out*. Half of what you say is bullshit. Stop hassling me and work it *out*. You're a very bright person, sound judgment, lots of practical good sense. When's the last time you went badly wrong?"

He's right. Why is she hassling him?

"You want to cut the man loose, cut him loose. If you don't, don't. You're not sure yet, give it a while, then ask yourself again. This is easy, compared to what's happening all around us. This is a *blessing*."

Right about that too.

"Furthermore, we're not letting anybody down."

"What's that got to do with my question?"

"Everything, Sarah. Isn't that what your daddy would say?"

In the morning Troy arrives right on schedule, but this time it's no comfort. This time, presumably due to his display of weakness yesterday and her refusal to make any reference to it having thrown a severe scare into him, he's like a torpedo heading toward her that she has no chance of outrunning.

"Now, Troy? *Now* is when you want to start with this? You can't be serious."

She knows what she feels, she is pretty sure what he feels, but she is so without defenses, so stripped down to bare metal, that she wants to sit on the floor and cry, both because she is allowing herself to be glad he's finally brought it into the open instead of forcing herself to not care and because she is so angry at him for coming at her when she has *zero* ability to cope, instead of *just fucking waiting*—he is surely as aware as she is that she has been slowly coming around, every day, for the last nine months—until a better time. It's not like either of them is going anywhere, is it?

"You saying I'm out of line?"

"Not at all. On a normal day in a normal week of a normal month I'd be all ears." She swears to god she has never in her fucking life said anything so straightforward about herself to anybody. She can feel her brain doing backflips. "But in the middle of *this*? Trucks stuffed with bodies and doctors sobbing and burning around the clock and George calling to beg us for a *cavity injector*? How on earth can you expect me to give it even a tiny part of the attention it deserves?"

"When is a better time to get close than when you're neck deep in the same shit?"

"How elegant," she replies, and instantly regrets it.

"Sorry, I'm plain-spoken."

"Also language."

That sigh. "The point is, Sarah, you make me smile. You make me smile all the time, except right now I can't fucking smile, but I sure hope to again someday. And I admire you more than ever. That's all I'm trying to tell you. No one chooses to fall in love. I already loved a lot about you, but loving you for the way you're

17

handling this brought it to another level. So I had to say something."

He turns his back and as she studies the stripes on his shirt and marvels at how moved she should be, how moved she is, by what he just said, she fights then gives in to the urge to go to him and touch his shoulder. While wondering how she can have known all along and still be so surprised.

Annie has her green tea. Sarah is on the cup of coffee three after the one she should have stopped with. And it's quiet, for once, for a miracle. The others are out, it's only the two of them, no one has called or come calling.

"What's up with your kids, Annie?" she asks out of nowhere.

"Why? What did you hear?"

"Relax! I'm just curious. Wondering how they are."

"They're good. It's been crazy with this 'remote' crap and no afterschool and Bill working longer hours than ever but they're good, thank god. They're taking it serious but not hard, if you know what I mean. We still have occasional fun and they're beating on each other same as always."

"See, that's what I wanted," she says, briefly closing her eyes. "To know they're good. And the same. That some good things are the same and not fucked over by this."

"Well, it's got a ways to go yet."

"I'm well aware."

"But they'll be okay." Suddenly Annie brightens, a little. She's not exactly smiling but the needle moves in the right direction. "Hey, did I tell you? Bill got into that program he was so excited about. It's been delayed, naturally, but eventually they'll run it and he'll be in."

"Wonderful. That's the science of evidence thing?"

18

"Yeah. All sorts of possibilities."

She actually laughs, leans back, closes her eyes again. "Possibilities. Exactly what we desperately need."

"Um, Sarah. Speaking of which."

They're open now.

"You know my father did the home's books before me. You probably know your dad was one of my favorite people growing up. Just to clarify my motives here."

She slowly nods, mystified.

"First of all, he's got an excellent head for business, for numbers and money. We've talked quite a bit and he really does. You were kind of limping along until the craziness hit and now that's not good enough. I'm not convinced you're headed for failure but I've been losing some sleep over it. With the two of you running the place together I think you'd have an excellent chance of getting back on a good footing."

This is unreal. Nobody overheard them this morning, she is utterly certain of that, and even more so that Troy didn't say anything. What got Annie into this? Psychic powers? Or has the whole crew been watching her soap opera unfold?

"Second, he's a good man. I'm married to one and I know what I'm talking about. I'm pretty damn sure he'll take good care of you. Not saying you're at that any port in a storm age but I'm totally not seeing the point in this business of proving your independence over and over again, year after year. You're a strong, smart woman who can absolutely look after herself but you're also entitled to companionship, to take a rest once in a while knowing someone has your back. And kids are good too."

She pauses; Sarah waits patiently.

"And he likes you. I mean he really likes you."

19

"Okay, Annie. You make a good case. I'll take a meeting with myself and hash it over."

Annie smiles a real smile, the broadest Sarah has seen on anyone in weeks, and then the phone and doorbell ring as one and wipe it away. Just like that. Annie heads for the desk so Sarah moves toward the foyer, though she feels not the slightest interest in bells of any kind—telephone, door, knell—aware as she is of why they're ringing.

Still, she won't forget the moment. "Death gives way to death, life to life," she says aloud, with confidence, not knowing why, not even knowing what she wants it to mean, certain it won't help but satisfied nonetheless, as if she has finally delivered the line she's been studying for weeks. For years. For as long as she can remember.

"Got that right," says Annie.

At the Riverside

"**If you think I'm letting a piece of shit like you** stop me coming in here, kid, you're crazy. Just keep your fucking mouth shut around me, understand?"

The man pushes past Max and starts for Cereals Hot and Cold, but he's just going through to the back of the store, where all the men like him go. Because that's where the beer is. Yeah, Max smelled it right away. He had some beer and wants more. "You know when someone's been drinking, right Max? Drinking alcohol, I mean." "Yes, mom." "So when they've been drinking alcohol you leave them alone, okay?"

No.

"I am not!" he says very loudly, as loudly as he can through his mask. "A piece of shit!"

Everyone is looking at him. Including the beer guy, who was a step or two into Cereals but has turned.

"I AM NOT A PIECE OF SHIT," he shouts.

Now more people are coming out of the aisles to stare at him. Cindy hurries over.

"Max, what's the—"

"Cindy, he said I was a piece of shit. Am I?"

"No of course not, Max, but you have to—"

"I. AM. NOT. A. PIECE. OF. SHIT." Max shouts, even louder than before. He is trembling, almost shaking, his whole body, like on that ride at Six Flags with Josie and her mom.

"You stay away from him, mister," says Cindy, stepping between Max and the man, who after standing there with his eyes bugging is finally heading their way. She glances over her shoulder. "Kyra, go get Mister Conklin. Go on, get him quick!"

"Step aside, girly," says the man. Cindy doesn't move.

"You're stupid," says Max. He hears surprised sounds from all around. "And mean and drunk and dirty." More gasps and as George practically jumps over the bakery counter and rushes toward them the drunk man shoves Cindy so hard she falls down and swings for Max's face.

But Max is quick. And the guy has been drinking beer. The fist hits him on the side of his head; it hurts, he almost loses his balance but finds it just in time to charge at the man as hard as he can, taking him by surprise and carrying him back into the end cap where the big squeeze bottles of mustard and ketchup and mayo are stacked. The whole display falls over. And so does the man. And so does Max.

Now I am dead, thinks Max as the man grabs his throat and chokes him hard, but George and Jenny pull his hands off while a couple of shoppers hold him down and another helps Max up. He sees Kyra helping Cindy, who is crying pretty loud. Every shopper in the store must be standing there looking.

Mister Conklin is *very* angry. Max has never seen him so angry, in fact he thinks he has never seen him angry at all, if this is what angry is. Also in fact, George has to hold Mister Conklin back as the three customers and Jenny—she's so strong! look at those muscles!—plus Franklin keep the man from running away, which he definitely wants to do. It needs all five of them, really, he's that big, and Max is glad to see two police officers coming down past the checkouts because it looks like he's about to get free.

Mister Conklin doesn't even notice the officers, he is way too busy yelling. "Who the hell do you think you are, attacking my workers? You won't be so goddamn brave when they throw you in the tank with the other drunks and tell them what you did!"

"Hey Joe, take it easy," says the older officer, putting his hand on Mister Conklin's shoulder.

"Do you know what this SOB *did*, Jerry?" asks Mister Conklin. "He hit Cindy and Max! Not me, not Jenny, Cindy and Max!" Max understands about Cindy, she's small, maybe weighs less than his youngest cousin Lucy. But doesn't Mister Conklin think he's tough?

"Anyone corroborate that?" asks the other officer, who has one blue glove hand on the guy's arm and the other on her gun in its holster. About ten people raise their hands—George, Franklin, Jenny, Kyra and Cindy, who is still crying, plus shoppers. "You're under arrest on suspicion—"

"No suspicion!" says Mister Conklin.

"—of simple assault." She glances at Mister Conklin and turns back to the man. The suspect, thinks Max. Or perpetrator. "You have the right to stay silent ..." she starts in and he sees the whole thing on TV, including the part where he charges a guy twice as big as him and pushes him into a pile of ketchup. He *is* tough! He thinks about his mom being proud of him, although she will also be upset.

He goes over to Cindy. "Thanks, Cindy," he says. "Thanks for protecting me."

She stops crying long enough to smile (her mask is off, in her hand) and say, "You sure didn't need it, Max. I always knew you were tough." He can't believe she said it! He wants to hug her but maybe it's better not to touch her right now. So he just smiles, but then can't stop himself from taking her hand and squeezing. She squeezes back.

His whole life, Max's mom has been telling him: "Different isn't better, different isn't worse, it's just different." He understands what she wants this to mean but has figured out some problems with it.

One: it sure looks better or worse sometimes. He's heard people from his big sister to Jenny to Mrs Logan next door say how good looking Ryan Gosling is. Isn't that better? Isn't it worse to be ugly?

Two: Max gets noticed for his face but there are guys just like him who don't. When they see him everyone is thinking "That boy has Down's" or "Down syndrome" or "he's developmentally disabled" (he hates that one) or yeah, "retard" or "moron". But with Isaiah, who's about the same as Max, it's way harder to tell.

Which means the people who do the little annoying things that make different worse do them not much to Isaiah but lots to Max. Like asking if he needs help with something a kid can do. Acting like his having a job is some big thing. Asking where he lives and making a face when he says "At home with my mom". Though he has kind of stopped caring, he agrees with his sister—when he tells her she usually says "That sucks!" and hugs him. Well, yeah.

But what bothers him most is pretending that people don't *like* different being worse. Because they really do. A lot of them, anyway. Enough for something to happen about every week at work. Usually it's small, like pointing or laughing when they think he's not looking. Once in a while it's bad. If the drunk man called him a piece of shit because of Down syndrome, Max would say it was bad but not the worst.

It became the worst because of what *he* did, though. The man did not actually hit him until Max called him stupid, mean, drunk, and dirty. And a guy like Max calling someone stupid is not so great. But it was definitely more good than bad. "Are you proud of yourself?" his mom asks once in a while. This time he pretty much is.

After it's finally over, after the officers talk to Max and Cindy and the people who saw it and then take the guy away (the woman tries to pay for a bag of chips at checkout three but Mister Conklin waves her through) and everyone uses a ton of sanitizer and George and practically the whole shift ask him and Cindy about twenty times are they sure they're OK and do they want to go home and the shoppers all finally go back to shopping and the workers to working, Mister Conklin waves to Max, who is bagging for Cindy—he really doesn't want to be anywhere except next to her—and points to his office. Max looks at Cindy, who says "Go Max, I'll bag, don't worry," so he does.

As he crosses the front of the store so he can get around past the ATM Max sees a little kid in shorts and an old SpongeBob t-shirt trying to put a quarter in the gumball machine. "Can I help?" Max asks and the kid holds out the quarter. Max fits it in the slot and says "Now turn the handle, like this," showing the right direction. He hears the clunk! he used to like so much as he walks away.

"Sit down, Max," says Mister Conklin, after taking his mask off, "and tell me what happened. From the beginning."

Max looks at the bottles of sanitizer and boxes of gloves and masks lined up on the table against the wall, where papers and family pictures used to be.

"Well, um, the guy came in and I said he had to have a mask —"

"We talked about that, right? How you're all going to come get me instead?"

"I know, but—"

"This is *exactly* why we made that rule, Max."

"No it isn't, Mister Conklin." What a day. First he fights a huge guy, then he watches an arrest and Cindy squeezes his hand, now he's arguing with his boss.

"I'm sorry, Max?"

"We didn't fight because I said that."

"So what happened?"

"He called me a piece of shit and I said I wasn't—"

"You were shouting."

"Okay, I shouted I wasn't. And he got mad and Cindy stopped him from hitting me and I said he was stupid and that's when he pushed her down and hit me."

Mister Conklin is staring like he's trying to decide about something. For a guy who felt so tough a little while ago Max isn't so sure now.

"Before I say anything else, Max, of course you are *not* a piece of shit, you're a human being and a better one than many. You're a fine young man and everyone who works or shops at this market is glad you're here."

"Thanks, Mister—"

"But it doesn't matter what people say to you. You are what you are and they can't change that. Only you can change it."

He is not sure he is getting this, so he just waits.

"Max, not only could that very large man have hurt you, he could have hurt Cindy. Maybe badly. What he said didn't matter, but that did."

Oh geez. He definitely didn't think of that. He definitely didn't think Cindy was crying and crying not because of what happened but because of what *might* have happened. Now that he has the tough is gone. And also the proud he didn't cry.

"It's okay, Max. I understand why you did it. But you're old enough to think about risk. You know what I mean by that?"

He nods his head, which is all he can do.

"It's *okay*, Max. This happened because he's an awful person, not from anything you did. And fortunately no one got hurt. But I want you to learn from this to think before you act. Even when you're excited."

Max nods again. He still doesn't want to talk.

"For example, say we're standing on the bridge near your house and I accidentally drop my wallet—"

"I get it, Mister Conklin. I really do."

"That's good, Max. That's excellent. I was already proud of you for sticking up for yourself and now I'm also proud you understood me so quickly." Mister Conklin is smiling now so Max tries to smile too.

"I'm not stupid, Mister Conklin," he says.

"I never, ever said you were, Max, and I've never thought it, either. Not even when you put up a whole shelf of cat food in the middle of housewares."

Oh boy. Max doesn't want to remember *that* right now. But when he looks again he gets that Mister Conklin is making a joke. He laughs, which is another surprise, laughing in this office, but, well, it really has been a crazy day.

Probably most people get called a piece of shit once in a while, Max figures. And have to decide whether to do something about it. Like that kid in sixth grade, Luca Ravazzolo, who kept getting suspended for saying things like that—a lot to Max, yeah, but also to girls, teachers, custodians, nearly everybody—until he got expelled. (Which must have made him very mad, although it shouldn't have surprised him, because he came in the next day and pulled over the huge old case with the trophies and stuff in the front hall so it made the worst sound ever when all that glass crashed to pieces.) Luca just liked to call people a piece of shit. A lot of guys bullied Max so he did too, but he didn't care who he said it to.

Sometimes it's the *situation*, not the *person*, his mom explained a long time ago, and Max thought about this for like a year until he got it. The drunk guy had a situation (needing beer) and probably would have been nasty to anyone who got in his way, even Jenny (he'd have been sorry). But this doesn't make Max any less sure he is *not a piece of shit* and or any less glad he finally said it out loud.

Back to bagging, the good part is Cindy smiling at him, like all the time. Too bad he can't see the whole smile but her eyes are enough. Even one smile from her is better than anything from anybody. She is one of the nice people at the store who are always looking after him, and he wishes he could look after them. Sure he does what they ask—he *jumps* to do it—but that isn't the same. They are like extra moms and dads. As he bags, though, and smiles back at Cindy and at Kyra when she comes past and does the champion thing over her head and the shoppers, Max sees that he didn't push the big man into the bottles because of the bad thing the man said. It was because of what he did to Cindy. Maybe that's why she is smiling so much?

The bad part is thinking about his mom, who Mister Conklin called before he spoke to Max. Because she is the one who is supposed to protect him, and when she wasn't there he did something risky. Mister Conklin is right, that's a good word, because, well, you do it and then it's just plain simple luck whether you get hurt. Like the time she saw him riding his bike without his helmet up on Pleasant Street, where people go so fast. Wow, did she shout and shout, and he got the point good and forever. You could do that and nothing would happen. Or you could be run over and killed. Just depending on the day.

Mister Conklin said he wished it was Max who told his mother but he had to call because she would hear it from someone else anyway and that person might not say "He's totally okay" and if they did she might not believe it. "I told her you were involved in a very short fight started by a customer," he said, "and that you weren't hurt *at all* and weren't upset, and that we talked about fighting being risky. That's it. She said in that case she would finish her shift and then come by." Which was good news. He *hates* making his mom leave work before she is supposed to. What if someone there needs her?

Being near her for so long, Max thinks a lot about Cindy and how special she is. He feels kind of the same way about Kyra too, she's really pretty and his age. But Cindy (who's a little older) is not like anyone. She is so nice and likes talking with him. She laughs at his jokes! And maybe she does look after him, but the way he jumps for her isn't like a guy jumping for his mom.

He would be very happy about protecting Jenny or George or Mister Conklin or Kimrika, they are all good friends and very nice to him and he would be proud to say he did. Or Kyra, with all that curly gold hair, always laughing and singing, and sometimes she pretends to tickle him or punches him on the arm even if she does have a tall football-type boyfriend who picks her up every day. But Cindy is different. Definitely a better different. If he had to choose someone to push a huge drunk guy into an end cap for, anyone in the whole world, it would be Cindy.

A few weeks ago when he was watching her change shelf tags while he mopped, hoping she wouldn't notice because it wasn't polite but he couldn't help it (and had to stop when Franklin said "I think you cleaned that spot pretty good by now Max") he thought of the girl with the braids. For the first time since who knows. The girl with the long shiny braids he liked so much for two whole grades—the way she looked, her voice when she walked with her friends, her dresses—but never even got to talk to. And remembering that now he can see it's the same difference. Cindy is a real friend and the girl was just someone Max watched from special ed, like looking at the TV, but it's the same. It's the same for everybody.

When Cindy goes on break Max switches to taking groceries out to cars. He is loading bags into the hatchback of the lady with the fancy glasses who is always trying to tip him (he says "no thank you" but she keeps trying) when he spots his mother parking their red 2008 Dodge Charger that needs new shocks way at the end of the first row, then getting out and waving to him. He's been pretty nervous for the last hour. As she walks toward where he is waiting with the empty cart, though, he can see she isn't angry, like with the bike thing; she has her tired after work face as usual. Standing and watching, the bright sun glaring in his eyes from behind her, Max feels a little afraid, so to calm down he looks around the lot to see if he can spot another Dodge. He's been feeling this way once in a while since that terrible week at the beginning of summer and it's funny he still does but, well, it's taking a long time to wear off is all.

Also funny is the way, when they go into the market—after she hugs him forever and checks him for bruises (noticing the small ones on his neck but not the big one under his hair) and asks him twenty times if he's OK and tells him to sit with her on the outside bench and explain what happened, the whole thing, and when he gets to the "stupid" part just nods, then when he says "I have to clock out" stands up and says "Oh, I'm going in, I need to see a couple of people"—everything seems far away. The crazy day is over, not that his mom meant to do that but he badly wants to go home. So he sits on the inside bench by the change counting machine and watches as she goes past the checkouts and Cindy waves her over and they talk and then hug for a long time, then Cindy points to Mister Conklin's office and his mom heads that way and goes in and closes the door. He looks at Cindy again and she smiles like she has for hours and though it still makes him happy and he still smiles back, he really does want to get out of there.

Finally she comes and he clocks out and they walk to the car together to head home. "What would you like for dinner, Max?" she asks as they wait to pull out of the lot. He doesn't care but she's trying to be nice.

"You said Cecily and Ryan were coming."

"She texted she's sorry but she's too tired. In her eighth month after all."

"What were you going to make, Ma?"

"Meatloaf. And mashed potatoes."

"Meatloaf sounds good."

The day still has plenty on it. If it was winter it would already be dark.

"Ma, since she gets so tired, maybe we could make dinner and take it over to their place and have it there."

"That's a lovely idea, Max. I'll suggest it."

"Or I could."

"Of course. Call her up and do that. Oh, meant to say, I need to stop at the PO."

"Sure."

They drive along silently for a little while. He listens to the air conditioner fan humming.

"Of course I've warned you about alcohol, Max," she says quietly as they pull slowly up to a yellow light while three cars that were behind them zoom through it in the other lane.

"Yeah."

"What have I told you?"

She's told him so many things it takes him a while to pick out a good one.

"That when some people drink alcohol the worst things about them get big and the best things get small."

"Right. That's right. So maybe this man is not violent like that when he's not drinking. But when he is—"

"Ma, I'm sorry, I wasn't thinking about him."

She glances at him just before the light turns green.

"Oh?"

"I was thinking about me. And people calling me a piece of shit."

"Have people called you that before, Max?"

"A lot, Ma." He is *sure* he told her about it at least a few times. "And lots of other nasty things that would make you mad."

"Like the r-word."

"That is nasty but it doesn't bother me anymore. They're just going to keep calling me that, I guess. You always told me people get scared looking at anyone they think they don't want to be, and it makes sense. But when they say 'stupid shit' or 'dickwad' or 'fucking loser'—I guess I got old enough to say no."

She is quiet for a long time. Maybe for once she gets that she doesn't know everything about what it's like to be Max.

Walking to the post office from the lot a few blocks over, she starts talking again. "So you think that's a good word Mister Conklin used, Max? I agree. Answering that man *was* risky and you shouldn't have done it at all, never mind shouting at him, I

34

didn't raise you to shout at people. You were upset with good reason, anyone could understand it, but anyone with good sense would tell you it was a bad idea." She stops in front of a coffee shop that smells very nice to search in her handbag for something, just a hanky it turns out. "And I know you know Mister Conklin is right, it's very important for you to *think* next time, and every time after that." She pulls her mask down and blows her nose, slowly and carefully, the way she always does.

"Like I told Mister Conklin, I get it, Ma. Yeah. But I have a question."

She starts walking again. "What is it, Max?"

"Shoppers who won't put on a mask. Even after they watch the news and read the sign, or Mister Conklin asks them to."

"Yes?"

"Well, that's risky. They *have* had time to think about it, but they do the risky thing anyway."

"Yes, I guess so."

"And the people at the hospital you tell me about, who go to parties and weddings and bars with no mask and get the virus."

"Oh my, yes. We have one of those now, Max. *And* we have someone who is terribly sick, who thought she was doing everything right. And it wouldn't help her at all to say, 'It's not your fault. You *were* doing everything right, but the man in bed seven, he was doing everything wrong, and it was someone like that who got you sick. It's their fault, not yours.' It was a hard, hard day. And tomorrow will be harder."

"I'm sorry, Ma."

"I know, dear."

"That's probably why you didn't go after me like you could have for shouting at a drunk guy and getting into a fight."

She laughs, which he guesses is what he wanted, and hugs him again outside the post office doors, where he is surprised there is no line. "You coming in?"

"I'll wait here." He used to like the PO. When he was nine, maybe.

As they start back to the car she is looking—what's the word, thinking about something else?—*distracted*, and sad too.

"Ma, I didn't say it yet."

"Say what, Max?"

"I didn't get to the end. Of what I wanted to ask you."

She looks at him. "Well, go ahead."

"You and Mister Conklin are right, it's a good idea to think first if something is risky. If I did that I would *never* have shouted, I would have gone for Mister Conklin."

"And remembering today will help you do that next time, right?"

"Still not the end, Ma."

"Okay."

"What I want to say is, the kind of risky where the person doesn't do it if they think about it first, it doesn't happen that much. There's a lot more of when the person totally knows and does it anyway."

He is surprised that she just keeps walking, a little faster actually, and nodding her head slightly.

"Like the people who get the virus from parties and bars. Like people who drink alcohol—who think about going to the store to buy alcohol, then do it, even when they haven't had any yet. And you're always telling me how some of them drive to bars *knowing* they will get drunk and then drive home."

"Yes, that's what some do."

"And there's lots of stuff people *hope* will turn out good but also know might turn out bad. Which is what risky means, isn't it? They think, maybe a lot, but they still do a risky thing."

Still nodding. Still walking a little faster all the time.

"Like, um, well, you and my dad."

She sighs her sigh, first time today. "Like me and your dad."

"I know you thought it would be good. And a lot of it is — you're a great mom for me and Cecily and we have a nice house and we are healthy now and you have a good job helping people."

She sighs again.

"But I don't have a dad. My dad went away and we don't know where he is and he isn't doing anything to help look after me. I know you didn't want that to happen. But it didn't happen because you called him stupid and pushed him into an end cap without thinking first, either."

She is walking very fast. And there are tears on her face and he feels really bad. But he is also remembering something he heard George tell Mister Conklin: "It needed to be said."

When Max gets to his room, finally — after talking a lot more with his mom during dinner and cleanup about people who drink and people who call you things and people who think the virus isn't real and even a little about his dad and what happened, though not enough, wondering the whole time if she will ever believe he knows something she doesn't, will ever be proud of him for something she didn't expect to be proud of him for — he lies on the bed and stares at the ceiling and asks himself, what's next? Does Max the Down syndrome boy work at the Riverside Market forever? Doing a good job and being looked after by nice people like George and Reynaldo and Mr. Conklin and Kimrika and yeah, Cindy, but never anything else?

His mother used to say he was going to college, like that girl in South Carolina they saw on TV years ago, she was saving up the money, and sure he made it into regular classes his last two years and passed every one of them—definitely *not stupid*, he might be the smartest Down syndrome around—but she hasn't mentioned it in a while. And he really doesn't know if he wants to. He doesn't know what it would be like, how it would change things, if people at college call you retard. That girl was named Hope and everyone thought that was so great but the thing about hope is that it maybe doesn't come true and then what? He hopes he can kiss Cindy one day but—not stupid, right?—he knows this is not going to happen, no matter how much she likes him and how much he jumps, and this makes him wish he could stop hoping. Good things you don't hope for that just happen, like today, those are much better anyway.

When his mom got the virus from the hospital in April and then he got it and they were both a little scared, when he got better but she got worse and they both got more scared because one of the other nurses actually died, when she was in the hospital as a patient for eight whole days and he stayed over Cecily and Ryan's garage and was *so fucking scared*, he didn't *hope* she would get better. He needed her, he *wanted* her to get better. Hoping doesn't mean anything. You have to know what you want. And what you're going to do. And he doesn't. That's what he learned today. Do one thing you wanted but didn't know you wanted and look for the next and nothing's there. Like he got a magic lamp and after one wish he can't think of any others, even a loaded-up cheeseburger or Six Flags.

That's what it's like to be Down syndrome at the Riverside. Not hoping *or* wanting. Just Max, with no next.

If he could be someplace where everyone's eyes look the same, where there is no such word as retard. Where no one is afraid of the virus or alcohol or guys like Luca Ravazzolo who are so afraid themselves. Where a Down syndrome boy could just say to a woman he works with "You are really special to me" and she would say "You are special to me too but you are Down syndrome and I am not so I can't kiss you. I can't do more than smile and once in a blue moon squeeze your hand" and it wouldn't be a problem, the boy could maybe start on a different hope and the woman would know she liked a Down syndrome and it could change something for her. But not for him.

His mother is knocking at the door. "Don't come in, Ma," he says.

"I never do unless you ask me to, Max. I haven't in years."

"What is it?"

He hears the sigh for the third time today, that he has wondered his whole life if it's a mom sigh or a Max's mom sigh—the situation or the person?—and then she's quiet. After a while she says, "I'm so glad you told everyone you're not a piece of shit, Max. I'm honestly very glad." He waits for more but that's it.

"Me too, Ma."

"Good night, Max."

"Good night."

Falling

There is definitely something wrong. Not coronavirus wrong, but metavirus. Or maybe ubervirus? Whatever, Tasha is doing her "force me to tell you" thing as part of her ongoing campaign to project a stable, solid, not-necessarily-happy-but-always-reasonably-calm image of herself. Which as she explains it comes from growing up amid the craziness of the Soviet Union/Russia and her parents' panicked flight from a chaotic, crime-ridden Saint Petersburg to resettlement in Allentown, Pennsylvania when she was 10.

"Luisa, are you even listening?"

"Of course. Honey, is that a *background*?" Tasha just laughs. "So you're not in the dining room?"

"Get real. You know I'm crammed up against a knee wall with roof spiders in my hair."

"Then why pretend it's the dining room?"

"Seriously? I was so embarrassed by this attic I blurred for the first two months. Then I noticed Gregory—you know, the guy who thinks he's a novelist?—had his work office. Which gave me the idea."

"How come I never saw it?"

"I don't hide anything from you, babe."

"No need to hide anything from *anyone*, Anastasia. The world may be four months into the toilet but you're sitting on a stable remote job and a very cool house with your healthy family safe inside it."

OK, that's it: telltale face twitches after *family*.

"Different toilet. From before the stinking virus."

No need to probe further because suddenly Tasha is crying, hard. After a few words of comfort she willingly tells all, which is that Faizan has been thinking he probably wants a divorce since way last November. Or that's when he first said so. On Thanksgiving to be exact.

"It was only the lockdown that stopped him moving out, Lu," she says through diminishing sobs, mopping with a tissue. "And then with the kids at home and so unstable he decided he'd stay put for a while. Just like that, like I'm nothing either way."

"Have you talked about it recently?"

"No, we don't fucking talk about it. He wants to fuck me every other day but not talk about it."

"Do you let him?"

"Hell yes. What do you think life would be like around here if I didn't?"

"Maybe he's changed his mind."

"Yeah. Well. We did talk about it the once. Not about *why* or what we might do to *fix things*, you understand, nothing unseemly like that, just enough for him to say that with the pandemic and all he has no idea how he feels about our marriage. Those were his exact words, Lu: 'At this point in time I really have no idea how I feel about our marriage.'"

She starts to speak but is interrupted by Tasha almost shouting, "After fifteen fucking years he has no fucking idea!"

"Oh honey. God damn *shit*."

"Do you have any idea what it's like to live with this on top of the rest of it?"

"Tashi, I am so sorry. It's wrong and horrible and you absolutely don't deserve it."

Tasha smiles, kind of, in that slight way she has and says, "Now I know why Mom wanted to go back to Saint Pete." Then she's sobbing again, even harder than before. "Jesus, don't tell anybody."

"Who do you think I am?"

After making Tasha agree to a walk in the evening, when Faizan and Dennis have come home, Luisa ends the zoom and glances at the clock. Behind again but who gives a rat's ass? She checks her personal email, the mommy address, work, the other personal and finds nothing that matters. Nothing on Messenger either.

When it hits her how disturbed she is by what she just heard she decides to finish the big table she's been working on before tackling the so-called urgent items. She finds Word tables soothing and doesn't care who knows it. As she rapidly merges and reformats she is forced to conclude that the answer to Tasha's question is *no idea whatsoever*. But though unburdened by marital strife (Dennis doesn't do strife) she too has personal worries piled on shared distress. Most are small, true; the bad stuff hasn't touched them yet, probably won't, and she is grateful. But try having a drug-abusing sister during a worldwide medical crisis, it's not exactly ropa vieja. Bee's been in and out of trouble, sometimes bad trouble, for years and Luisa's scared to death she will catch it and die alone. And her problem is bigger than just the drugs; no one can believe that a delicately beautiful Chinese woman with an unplaceable accent is an addict to begin with, and when they learn that her full name is Beatriz Marrero and she was adopted at thirteen months from a Shanghai orphanage by a

Cuban American family they back away, as if she's too outlandish to be saved. This is tough enough in the best of times but with very serious shit going on all over what chance does a woman who's reflexively labeled *beyond help* have of getting any?

Well, right now it's Tashi who's in the shit. Saving the table and moving on to her many mutually contradictory lists, it comes to her in her—what? empathy? anger? disgust?—that maybe Faizan's just out of his Pakistani mind. And always has been. It's so fucking hard to tell with all the boundaries blurred. Since disorientation settled in hard in April she has often recalled (OK, been haunted by) her college roommate's words over frozen daiquiris at a DFW bar the August before last, she heading home from a funeral and ambitious Melly en route to a diplomatic post in India: "Yeah, my friends and I laugh our butts off comparing Nigerian parent stories. But I finally see the truth about mine—it's not that they're Nigerian, it's that they're nuts! Personally nuts." She's been reliving, for the first time in years, the disorienting childhood trips to Little Havana, where her mami and papi seemed so different, almost like strangers; she has at last begun to appreciate that Tasha's struggles are due in part to her oddball origins obscuring her true attributes, as if she's behind an Instagram filter. And late at night, when she can't sleep—which is getting to be all the time—she obsessively develops her enduring fantasy of "explaining" her sister to some reluctant social worker (like that would help!). "It's not where she comes from or who raised her," she aches to say. "It's *just Bee*. She's wildly generous, vain, a great salsa dancer, an opioid addict. Like Jane Smith from West Virginia." Or Faizan in a parallel reality. Or Luisa.

When she was young, confusion was all to the good. Now she is not so sure. Then it was exciting that her marriage was "mixed" and she delighted in challenging friends, acquaintances, strangers at parties over "race" and "subculture". For Luisa at 24 having unimpeachable POC bona fides while experiencing many of the perks of whiteness was the best of both worlds; from one day to the next she was reliably grateful to have a basis for engaging with pretty much anybody who was next to her. Now the very idea often makes her cringe.

At some point in their early months together Dennis, mister sufficient unto himself, made reference to her "affinity for difference" and they laughed themselves nearly to death. His parents' friends were all old-line WASPs, hers likewise swam the Cuban exile sea but while he found this utterly normal she longed for alternatives. Throughout the early years they both enjoyed the tension—it was great fun coming up with the white girl pop/Latin blast playlist for their wedding; in bed he would whisper things like "this is how the gringos do it" when he wanted to push her over the edge—but the corollary (who cares?) was always lurking. And as her cheerful preoccupation was superseded by discontented obsession she somehow found herself being constantly let down.

"Don't want to minimize your concerns, *hermosita*, but you're not so special, just a little oversensitive," Dennis told her near the beginning of their first big multiday blowup, which didn't happen (he was a truly mild man and she dearly loved him for it) until just before their third anniversary. "Everyone deals with that stuff. Try being from an old, down on its luck New England family that no one particularly wants around anymore. Do I look like I have a 'community'?"

Glancing at the clock she sees that the closest thing he's got— his kids—will be home from "Tuesday in-person activities" (didn't they used to call it "day camp"?) before she knows it, so she'd better decide what she wants to accomplish (how 'bout that analytics report?) by dinner-making time. Many women have adapted well to the "hybrid" life, quite a few apparently prefer it, but she's a one role at a time kind of gal. Whose *affinity for difference* (when he says it nowadays it verges on derision) has lately homed disturbingly in on the mystery of how she came to be Luisa: the darkish-skinned Latina daughter of Maricela and Lazaro with a one-off sister, almost zero Latinx associates of any kind, a fair-haired gin-drinking Mayflower-descended spouse who builds gardens for rich people and has parents who still dignify him with his middle name (Henry) while everyone else (except Luisa) calls him Denny, and a best friend whose *authentically* mixed marriage and Jewish-Muslim kids with skin like a golden glow represent the only interruption in a stiflingly mundane wasteland of disinterest. Plus a black work husband. Is it all at bottom deliberate, some sort of overwrought *arrangement*? Maybe she's the one who's nuts!

Take Deandre: he certainly *is* different, although it's hard to pin down. Growing up she didn't know any African Americans well and as Deandre once described it his life was "pretty much all black, all the time" until he started college. On the other hand they have a number of coworkers (all non-Hispanic whites) whom she suspects of lumping them together because they aren't non-Hispanic whites, and in truth there's something to this; she has laughed with him many times about things that would be awkward or worse to even discuss with most of their colleagues, never mind poke fun at.

And then there's the affinity. When it came to her that she might be considered a "work wife" she rejected it out of hand as one of those trite, irksome trivializations (like "bucket list") but once she gave in and googled she chanced on someone's definition—"a platonic friendship with a work colleague characterized by a close emotional bond, high levels of disclosure and support, and mutual trust, loyalty, and respect"—that while a bit over the top was a not unrewarding, substantive, reasonably accurate description of their relationship. Plus when she sent the link to Deandre the euphemism "high level of disclosure" for "blabbing without restraint" amused him as much as it had her.

Imagine her surprise! Her thoughts have again settled on D, which happens every fucking day. Well didn't she spend her work weeks for almost a year looking forward to his presence? Didn't they go on lunchtime walks every so often, stop by each other's cubes all the time, invariably find a few minutes at their department's frequent social events to stand together and laugh or whisper or raise eyebrows, depending?

Ping! An email from Tasha: **thank you, dear friend, i don't deserve you** (Tashi uses very few capitals) with an elaborate watercolor of roses. **Ha ha we deserve each other!** Luisa writes, adding **I'm so happy to be able to help** before sending.

The bottom line is it's not trivial at all. A work (nonfucking) marriage is based on intimacy without dependence and all the consequent vulnerability; you can ask for advice, get something off your chest without the minefield of risk attendant on a fucking marriage. She and Deandre hid nothing from each other. Of course there are lines around the fucking spouses—around certain characteristics of the fucking spouses and their interactions with same, certain feelings, certain experiences—that are never to be crossed, but everything else is fair game.

And she's not thinking "intimacy" in the broader sense; she would never deny that simple attraction was her main reason for persistently chatting him up in the kitchen and lobby until he caught on that she wasn't some would-be Karen who wanted to feel his hair. And soon enough the feeling was definitely mutual, and the flirting made for good clean fun.

Which doesn't translate too well to the screen, she's well aware. But that's not sufficient to explain where it went! As the weather warmed and she heard from him less and missed him more, experiencing all the wounded longing of a teenager who counts the hours until her boyfriend returns from summer camp while wondering every day why he doesn't write, she began to question whether they'd been friends at all. And the fuzzier her memories got the harder they were to qualify. She is not yet certain she has become a work widow but is definitely studying for the role.

And god damn it, after months, *months* of this, in light of Deandre's painful withdrawal and Dennis giving her exactly the same attention as always despite a global panic, she honestly doesn't know if she feels a "high level of loyalty" to either of them. To *anyone*. Ever. Yes, she wants to fuck Deandre. Or did until recently. And she was crazy hot for Dennis for a long, long time. But sooner or later that all drains away, doesn't it?

By the time Messenger rings her daily self-mortification has for the zillionth time led her down the rathole of recalling their very spouselike squabble (*more like quarrel, or let's just say fight*) a couple of weeks before the lockdown, about her reference to his "black name" — "I keep telling you I get all that, Deandre, it's the same for us isn't it?" "Then why the fuck would you say something you understood to be offensive?" "Not sure. Because I thought you'd just laugh instead of pitching a total fit?" — and asking, for the equally zillionth, if it could possibly be the reason it all seems to have evaporated. Or a clue that it had long before. Despite her compulsive self-distraction she's finally getting on with the stupid report so *don't even look, it's just Tasha begging off*. But she can't help checking and when she does it's D.

you there? alone?

Within roughly twenty seconds she manages to review maybe forty possible responses, including not answering at all — *how long has it been?* — and settles for the safest.

yes
until?

30-40 max

And then radio silence. Although she sits there staring for what is quite a while, considering. And when the doorbell rings about five minutes after that, as much as she'd like to pretend she doesn't know who it is her knees go weak. Still she manages to cross the living room, put on the "greeting random visitors" mask she keeps in the hall, and pull open the door.

It is. It really is. She's amazed he's standing there, equally astonished she can accept it so readily.

"Good to see you, D," she says as she steps into the surprisingly cool sunshine, arms crossed. "What's the occasion?"

His eyes are fixed on her. "Pandemic Tuesday?"

"Very good, you know the day of the week. Both feet on the ground. I like that. And look at you, so presentable."

The furrowed brow of his pretend frown is something she truly, dearly loves.

"Ever see me when I wasn't?"

She does actually, she loves his frowns and his caring heart, she treasures the memories of laughter but quite suddenly and very emphatically she is not in the mood for banter.

"Deandre, what the fuck are you doing here?"

"I have something to tell you. In person. It would be horrible not to."

She feels so tenderly toward him. Way more than she should. It suddenly registers that his mask is jet black. *The one for funerals.*

"Go ahead then."

"We're moving away."

"What? I'm sorry?"

"To Georgia. To be close to Luna's family. Her mom's old and sick. She misses her sisters and wants the kids to know their cousins."

He pauses, perhaps giving her a chance to react to his well-practiced recitation, but gauges the stillness of her face for only a second before continuing. "She's been pushing for it a long time and decided this"—he gestures, as if it doesn't matter whether he means *this viral hell* or just *this*—"was the moment."

"*Now?*"

He looks down, scratches his ear, nods. "And I lucked into a really good job. The network security space we talked about."

It's all she can do to keep herself from turning around, going inside, slamming the door with all her strength.

"When?"

"End of next week."

She would definitely flee if she wasn't afraid of falling.

"Why haven't you told me? This must have been in the works for months."

"Because *I didn't want to*, Luisa. Why do you think?"

It's one thing to lose a friend to passing chaos, she feels a strong need to explain, and assume that when the emergency ends, when things are as "back to normal" as they're going to get, they will return. It's another when the loss becomes permanent. Another entirely.

"Because I don't want to leave you."

"But you are."

He looks deep into her eyes for longer than he ever, ever has. "I am."

It's tough enough, even when you know it's temporary, to be limited to the personal presence of your delightful but needy kids, your generally considerate, cheerful, hard-working but increasingly distant husband, your cryptically fragile best friend and her question mark of a spouse and their strangely independent offspring with whom you and yours are in some kind of bastard "pod", phone calls to Hialeah to scold your parents for their lack of caution in a state apparently run by staggeringly irresponsible children, video calls with your sister who might or might not be on drugs and might answer, if she does at all, in her living room or bathroom or in the stairwell or on the roof—any of those at any hour though no fucking clue as to why—and refuses to acknowledge that you are terrified for her, the grocery employees you recognize from the mask up or by body shape, the mail carrier who always, *always* comments on the weather. Tough enough even knowing that on some blessed day there will be other resources to fall back on. It is different—it is hard, untenably hard—to abruptly embrace the fact that on that day you will also walk into a house that once was home to find it stripped of all furnishings, bereft.

It's already tricky to focus. Too sudden. Too much to ask.

"Well," she says. "I will miss you. I will miss you *terribly*. It's really difficult to catch up to this, Deandre, but I think I get it. I'll never see you again, will I?"

He looks—no, he *is*, she knows he is—more miserable than she thought he could look. Could be. One of the things she'd admired was his determined enthusiasm, his refusal to be brought down by anything thrown in his path, but like all virtues it apparently has its limits.

"I'm so sorry, Luisa." And he is, she knows he is. It's as if his sorrow is touching hers, that's how well she knows it. If he had a choice he would not let this happen. But he doesn't. No one ever does.

"Goodbye, Deandre," she says, reaching for the door as she steps back into the hall, getting a good grip. "I'll never forget you." And then, preparing to do just that, she closes it forever.

What You Can't Give Me

What You Can't Give Me

G ene is shouting at her from clear across the restaurant. "Hey Nicky, you charging the candles?" Which is truly weird. It was the very first job he gave her, she's done it every night since then except when indoor was banned, he's never mentioned it before.

"Charging the candles" is rounding them up at closing, racking their tumblers for the dishwasher, cleaning them as needed (she is no longer surprised by how much food some people manage to fling into a three-inch tumbler eight inches from their plates) and putting them in their charging trays. So someone else can set them out for the next day's dinner service, it used to be, almost always one of the men. And she could understand that, really. There are usually some customers in the house and a lot of them like to watch the women work—especially when it involves reaching past them to put something on the table—but it's obviously a skill thing; guys can definitely center a fake candle in a round tumbler on a square table way better than girls. There being no guys left except Gene, however, he's forced to rely on her.

It's also odd and very Gene that when the so-called patio opened he just left them in back. She wanted to ask if she could go get them but he'd been so touchy and crabby since Firing Day, telling him what to do was clearly a foolish risk.

There are times when she wonders—standing behind the bar, for instance, watching the masked, unhappy people hurry by—do they worry? The real victims come first, of course, the ones on the suffering heap. But there ought to be some pity left for her and the others. Winter will be here before they know it.

She started in retail food service at sixteen. She's twenty-two now. So it's been almost six years, which she knows doesn't sound too long if you're fifty and work in an office but really is pretty long at her age. Especially in food service. As a woman. With breasts. As any such person can tell you.

When she was thirteen her father showed her a week's worth of strips from a newspaper comic. It started with this gal who waited tables in her old man's restaurant asking her boyfriend's visiting mother, "How do you like my twenty percent top?" Of course the mom (who worked in an office) didn't get it so she explained that when she wore it she got twenty percent more tips. It went on like that through the week, with the girlfriend and the boyfriend and the boyfriend's parents and the girlfriend's dad all having their say about whether she should wear it. And in the last panel of the last strip she told the mother, "You should see my forty percent top!"

Did her father guess she'd end up like this? She figures he was probably trying to say something broader but either way here she is, wearing her own twenty percent tops from time to time. One she's pretty sure is closer to thirty-three, actually; the rest she hasn't bothered to calculate.

It's not like anyone notices it's only young women now. But if they did, seeing any of them with Gene would explain it. He likes having them around. That's why he hired them in the first place.

It was very far from her favorite when Janina was crying and she was crying and she was totally ready to say "Keep her, I'll go" except then they'd both have taken a walk. That was a bad day, Janina and Eddie and Javon all at once after Lambert the week before. Of course it was Gene's call, and she and Skippy and Sahaja also had rent coming due; welcome to the world of paid employment. But it was a very bad day.

Her dad told her once that when he was young his mother almost had to slap him to get him to see how much women's lives sucked, which he later felt should have been obvious. And sure enough, some of the stuff she's read and seen is mind-blowing. Like women were, well, some sort of *domestic animal*.

He also wanted to make it clear that though there are plenty of men who at least try to respect women, there are a lot more who only talk a good game and a whole big bunch who don't remotely give a shit. And the ones who are trying are still men, right? Most are more or less covered by a quote she once saw, from Simone de Beauvoir: "Men are human beings and women are females, and when women behave like human beings they're accused of trying to be male." She'd say Simone pretty much nailed it there.

The truth as she's seen it for years is that even the caring, respectful guys are way more ignorant about women than they realize. In fact she sometimes thinks it's the ones who aren't so fucking sympathetic who get it the most, Gene being a case in point. He's totally aware they have an arrangement; he keeps money in her pocket and she acts like they're *good* friends—she jokes with him, does him little favors, touches him sometimes and lets him touch her (like, including her butt now and then). Most

59

likely he even knows that telling himself he's not fucking her only because he's too decent to cheat on his wife is total make believe. And while she's sure he'd happily go along if one of them willingly took him into the office and did him a *major* favor, wife or no wife, and gladly reward that person with extra hours or whatever it was she wanted, Nicky is reasonably confident that he will never assault her or make her an offer she can't refuse. Which is one reason she stays.

Watching a tipsy and very likable party of three older couples during the minute she has to rest before going back to get their orders, she feels (as she does almost all of her working minutes) like part of the background. Which is natural enough; they came for the company, the booze and the food, not the help. But as they drink and laugh together she wonders if any of them have a daughter like her, who works in a different setting and makes a lot more money but still tells them she feels like part of the background.

It was different in spring; things were bad and getting worse until the takeout thing fired massively up and there they were in the spotlight. It was funny how customers they didn't notice much before looked like angels in April and May, showing up for their bag twice a week, asking how they were doing and giving them huge tips. She wanted to come around the plexi and hug them sometimes. And when the city handed over a piece of the street in June they were right away turning at least two or three covers a night out there, contagion be damned.

The thing is, though, while it's nice they want her to keep her job and the place to stay in business, almost none of them realize what a shit line of work it is. Even without a pandemic.

Her father passed in February, suddenly and at peace, just before everything went south. When it comes up she has to carefully explain that it wasn't the virus and watch the other party lose interest. It was the biggest surprise of her life but though this one resident took her aside and said something about a-fib and maybe a clot that should have been treated she turned down the autopsy, he was dead and always would be and it was just one of those crap things in life that keep happening no matter what else is going on.

He was forty-seven when she was born and her mother was twenty-eight. They weren't married or anything close; her mother apparently said "I'm Tina!" (imagine having a mother named Tina) in the produce section of the old Harvest co-op and picked him up right there and then. A year later she disappeared forever, a couple weeks after they brought infant Nicole back from the hospital, although she did leave a bunch of formula in the kitchen and this note: "You're already a better parent than I will ever be." How all of this could have happened—a freakishly careful guy like him shacking up on a whim with a radically younger woman and knocking her up without benefit of matrimony, somehow taking it all in stride and raising the kid by himself as if it was the most natural thing in the world, beaming like all the younger dads at her high school graduation—is a puzzle at best.

She does have a theory she has no way to justify: that her mom was the only woman he ever went to bed with, the only one who could push past his obsessive good behavior, the only one he ever loved, and it makes her cry. But that's when she can hear him saying, very clearly, "You're okay, Nicole. And so am I; I have you."

Out on the patio one warm evening, just after Independence Day, a chunky bearded guy with a slightly too-loud voice is insisting that #metoo is all about privileged women, not the ones with two jobs and kids who get backed into the freezer by the boss and have no option but going to their knees and getting it over with. Which very much gets her attention. One of the women he's with says sure, it's always the privileged who have the leeway to make a fuss and Nicky's thinking she has a point until he says oh yeah? So it was a bunch of privileged black folks telling the New Yorker how those white guys lynched their fourteen year old and they just froze? It gets quite, well, animated, to the extent that people at other tables are looking over and one tall coder type tries to go tell them to shut the fuck up except his boyfriend is holding onto his belt.

She spends the rest of her shift thinking about it, admiring beard guy for his bluntness even if he did make it too simple, remembering how astonished she was that so many men were truly shocked, blown away, because somehow they'd had no idea. Of course countless guys young and old were watching Weinstein and then Kavanaugh and thinking about that drunk girl they pretty much forced to blow them in high school or college and does she remember (they bet their ass she does) and does she know where they are and is she putting that shit on facebook *right now*? But she also saw that when the clean ones, the relative innocents, began to grasp just how much women were taking— when they started to actually get the *go home, cry all night, come to work the next day pretending it never happened* thing—it predictably made them angry to find out they'd been so clueless.

And after midnight, making tea before bed, she decides her father would have liked the guy's perspective but hated his style. He was very responsible and never loud, almost never sarcastic and gave a lot of people, including her, far more benefit of the doubt than they were entitled to. And now he's dead and gone while some asshole who got COVID at a maskless dive in

Arkansas and lay for a couple weeks in a hospital trying to infect the people who were saving his life is still out there being loud, sarcastic and irresponsible while giving no one the benefit of anything.

It's a couple weeks later that Jesse shows up. Things are still fairly stressed. The panic is long over, toilet paper is back in stock and indoor is open just about everywhere but lots of people are still afraid, still wanting the curbside thing, still touchy about space in line at the market never mind a restaurant dining room.

It's a terrible night, no hope for the patio, so Sahaja goes home leaving Nicky and Skip. When she comes back from the kitchen she finds him standing there with his sneakers completely soaked.

"Can I order takeout and wait for it?"

"Sure," she tells him, leaning over the bar to point out the huge blown up menu Gene posted on the wall. "As long as you keep your mask on and maybe hang in the corner so you don't spook the other customers." He looks out at the rain. "People still want their treats," she says, gesturing toward the table with several bags lined up. While he studies the menu she gives him a once over.

"Can I just tell you my order?"

"Of course, why not?"

"The last place wanted me to use their 'platform' on my phone."

She laughs. "I'll bet it was the Baltic Diner." He nods. "Oh, Evgeny is *crazy*. Excellent cook, good guy, but totally nuts. Just tell me what you want."

After all the bags are picked up she talks with him for a bit while the Skipster makes his food. From a distance of course.

She's had her share of attention—way more if she's honest, which it's tough to be on the subject—but has avoided taking advantage, knowing as she does that it's nothing she earned. (The one time she dared ask her dad what her mom looked like he just smiled.) So she's not all that experienced. Not innocent by any means but not a good time girl either. Not yet anyway.

If he'd tried to influence her in that area it might have been different. She asked his advice a couple times and he helped her decide about birth control but in general seemed content to let things develop. In other words he trusted her. She can hear that clearly too: "I trust you, Nicole." "I believe in you." She's still not so sure all this confidence was justified.

Jesse is nothing special but that's what she likes about him. He isn't writing a novel or a screenplay. He isn't planning a "trek" from Lithuania to Vietnam. He has some job he won't discuss except he's glad to still have it.

One slow Thursday evening he's sitting on the patio and she's standing like she's taking his order but really he's saying, "It's one of those 'I feel like getting in the car—"

"Do you even have a car?"

He chuckles. "'Like getting in the car, driving to Schenectady and finding a one-room apartment and a job in a grocery' kind of days."

"That paints a very clear picture."

"And making friends with someone who washes dishes in a bar so I can sit in the alley behind on a milk crate drinking beer from a paper sack, listening to the music and talking to them when they come out to smoke."

Honestly, she wishes she could put a heart on it.

They go on a lot of walks, really a lot. Week after week. What else can they do? An occasional jazz club or movie would be nice but go pound sand as her dad liked to say. Plus the exercise is good and even better they can talk. Which gives her reason to believe it's not her looks he's most into.

Late one evening he asks, "When you first go out with a guy, or meet one somewhere, is it always the same small talk?" This is after they start holding hands. Not for the whole walk, often not for very long, but steadily more as the days go by. No hugging and like that though, only the hands.

"Afraid so," she says. "And small is exactly right."

"Where are you from et cetera?"

"Yeah."

"But not 'do you feel safe at work?'"

"Never."

"Or 'what's it like to be blonde and stacked?'"

She looks at him and he's grinning.

"That would be a first."

"Not that I'm asking you now."

"Not that I'd tell you. Until I know you a lot better."

They walk another half block. "Nicole," he says, "I think you're a very grounded person. I mean you totally know which end is up."

She is surprised to be so touched. "I'm glad."

"How'd you get that way?"

"My father," she says. "He insisted."

"Sounds like an unusual man."

"Definitely out of the ordinary."

"I'd like to meet him some day."

Is it him or herself she doesn't have the heart to tell?

65

She quickly got into the habit of simply saying "My dad died" and leaving it there. She wanted to do better but he was all she had and it was very fucking hard, not remotely like anything she ever went through. And to realize a few weeks after he passed that they were heading into an international calamity was disorienting and sharply painful—like carefully stepping back off the lowest rung on a ladder and discovering it was actually one higher.

He didn't suffer, she told him how much she loved him literally the day before, it turned out (once she easily located the IMPORTANT PAPERS INCL WILL folder in one of his desk drawers) that he'd long since arranged everything to make it as easy on her as possible. Despite all this she wept for days but eventually began to feel better; she had a job and a couple friends and all the time in the world to grieve. And then the shadow of doom hit everyone.

One Friday Jesse doesn't show. They have their usual plan for a walk but Nicky's thinking about taking him to her apartment instead. Both her roommates are away so if he's amenable there'll be no obstacle. Though all they've done is hold hands she's hoping he'll take her to bed. Or allow himself to be taken. Partly for physical reasons but more because she's beginning to get a glimpse of an adult relationship and wants to nail it down a little.

When he doesn't arrive at the usual time she's annoyed. Then worried. Then angry and wondering, how the fuck did that happen? It's half past obvious she cares much more than she knew. In fact it feels like the day she decided out of the blue, walking home from basketball practice, that Jimmy would get her cherry and they'd live happily ever after. But she's not a stupid kid anymore.

She slams all the way back to worried, though, when he finally arrives. He looks *terrible*. She quickly locks the back door and punches in the code, then throws her arms around him and holds tight. And after a while he holds her too. They stand like that for a long time, her head on his shoulder, and at last she feels him relax, by no means all the way but it's a start.

She turns toward the street and puts her arm around his waist, begins walking him up the alley. She counts *one, two, three* and then his goes around her as well. When they reach the sidewalk they turn left, which just so happens to be what she wanted.

"Um, Jesse, I'm fairly beat," she says, "and I'm guessing a drink and a comfortable chair wouldn't do you any harm. Maybe we could head to my apartment and, you know, talk while *not* walking for a change."

"Alone?"

"Yeah. Long story but yeah."

"Okay, that sounds nice. But I have to ask you something. Before I lose my nerve."

"Before you what?"

"You'll understand when I ask."

"So hit me already."

"I need seven hundred dollars. And I need it soon."

For a moment she wants to take her arm back; she's glad she doesn't follow through but she is shaken.

"I have nowhere to turn."

"I know the feeling."

"Do you? This is mortifying, Nicole, and I would so much rather skip it."

"But you have nowhere to turn. I get it, Jesse. And I don't mind your asking *at all*. Okay?"

"Okay. But?"

She stops and steps away so she can look him in the eye.

"My father told me not to lend money. Except *maybe* to someone very, very close."

"I totally understand that position."

"And it's hard for me to go against his advice on something like this. I mean it's hard."

"I get that too."

"But," she says, turning toward her apartment and putting her arm back around him.

They take a few silent steps. "Again, but?"

"But maybe. Maybe, okay?"

"Listen, I don't want to push you. In fact this may be more about reminding myself there's actually someone I can ask."

"I'm not 'someone', I'm your friend. And you wouldn't ask if you didn't have to."

"That's true."

"So you asked a friend. Big deal. It's only money," she says, smiling at him (bravely she hopes).

"That you saved by working hard."

"I have some by way of my dad."

"Who said you shouldn't lend it to me."

"Jesse, dear," she says, "will you shut the fuck up now and let me have the last word? Which is *maybe*."

"Good enough."

She's the skeptical type and is in mourning on top of it. But Jesse, she now realizes, has been getting past all that for weeks. And once she opens a couple of beers and whips up some garlic pasta and sets him on the sofa and puts on netflix and gradually, *very* slowly and gradually and carefully works herself closer as they watch until she is at long last lying back in his arms, it all seems to dissolve and drain away. She's done OK by him this evening, taken care of him a little, and has already decided he'll get his loan so rewarding herself maybe? With crazy thoughts like, *you could be happy.* Like, *you don't always have to worry about other people's motives.* And most of all an urge for change, which she can honestly imagine being an improvement. Nothing too specific; it's not like she's thinking about finding a no butt touching job or going to school. She's simply open for once, open to the potential of what she might call blessings if she could admit they existed. She leans back and looks into his eyes.

There have been a couple times when she's gone to kiss someone and knew in the first half second they didn't want it. But having it happen with Jesse is like walking into a wall. And for whatever reason—that would be reasons, so many reasons, because you can't really become less of a child in the time it takes to make and eat noodles and watch a mediocre movie—instead of giving herself a minute and room to maneuver, she takes it hard.

"What the fuck?"

"Sorry?" He leans away, startled, and she jumps to her feet.

"I said what the *fuck.* Are you kidding me?"

"Whoa, Nicky. Calm down."

"Don't give me that shit. What's the problem here Jesse?"

He stares like he's confused, then disappointed, then checking out a gorilla. Finally he stands and goes to the window, which somehow makes her angrier. She's also at the same time actually *trying* to calm down but it's like groping for a brake pedal that's just not there.

"You making assumptions, maybe?" he says at last. "Taking too much for granted?"

"What's the problem with my fucking assumptions, then?"

"It's complicated."

"Meaning you're gay? Or asexual?" She can't even pity herself, it's so pathetic.

He faces her again and his expression isn't hostile or even disgusted, just pained. "Oh Nicole."

But he's looking at her now so she plays her ace, or what feels like it in the moment: she takes off her shirt. Which turns out to be way more pathetic than the other. And beyond pity, really.

"Nicky," he says at last, "hanging with you has been great. It was so nice to be close to you just now." He turns back to the window and only then does she feel exposed. "But *I don't want to fuck you.* Not now and probably not ever, after this."

As he walks to the door and puts his hand on the knob she feels her face go red, pictures herself pleading. His voice gets lower but more urgent. "In the morning I'll be sorry I said that, I suppose. I wish we could go on like before, looking forward to it maybe happening someday. But of course you had to force things. I may never get another chance with a girl like you"—she hasn't a clue if this is sarcastic, and just then notices his tears—"but I do have some pride. Much as that might surprise you."

She wants so badly to speak, she is desperately trying, but at the very moment she forces out "Please wait, Jesse" he turns his back one last time. "In case you weren't notified," he says to the door, calmly but very firmly, "we don't always get what we want." Then he opens it and if he hears her "I'm sorry" it doesn't stop him. She listens to his footsteps in the hall and then nothing.

And after a time, quite a long time in fact, spent lying on her bed—thinking of very little at first or at least trying to, wondering if it's real life or circumstances or maybe something seriously, badly wrong with her that she's been ignoring for years, wanting a great deal to believe that her father (whose name, if anyone cares, if Tina even bothered to remember it, was *Jasper*) will somehow soon arrive, though as Jesse noted wanting's sure as fuck not enough and it's not at all clear what he could offer on this occasion—she rises and goes out, walks down to the restaurant, turns off the alarm (*fuck* Gene and the text he'll get), unlocks the door and goes in. And though she considers doing some damage (the so-called candles, for instance, she could start with those) in the end she settles for writing it on the bathroom wall with the lipstick Janina left, pausing at first for composition and then putting one sentence after another, unhurried, reflective, not even slightly surprised that for once, for once in her fucking *life* she's using up all the available space:

There's a pandemic. And nowhere to hide. So cry all night and come back here tomorrow. And pretend it never happened.

And what, she wants to ask of whoever isn't there, are her alternatives?

What You Can't Give Me

I AM NOT ASYMPTOMATIC

S he was glad, actually. It pained her, it was mortifying to admit even to herself, but she was glad there would be no funeral. Aside from never having seen the point anyway it meant she would avoid having to listen to Rudy's bullshit. After roughly fifty years of it she should have been immune and until recently maybe she was, but the little voice inside that long ago started whispering "you don't have to take this" had lately, due to circumstances, become loud and insistent. And the prospect of having to put up with, in particular, *again*, his lecture about how their mother's death after she'd been needlessly exposed to COVID was "just one of those things" that was "nobody's fault" and "would have been something else" if she hadn't been infected or if the virus weren't around, even "a relief in some ways" because she'd passed quickly and painlessly instead of becoming ill with something "much harder on everyone" months or years later was way, way too much to even contemplate at this point. In fact if she were required to hear it in person she would be forced to punch him in his big fat face, so it was a good thing she wouldn't be.

To be fair—it was a phrase her son used, although sometimes he said "To be honest"—well, to be honest, some of the problem with Rudy (not all, but some) was that for whatever reason, everything she disliked about men seemed to remind her of him, whether he was guilty of it or not. For example, her brother had always been a big interrupter of women, so it wasn't too surprising that whenever some yappy guy cut her off she thought of him. But as it happened she disliked much more the way a lot of men, when informed that they were wrong, were somehow prepared with a revision of context that made them right again. Such as "But if we go via the parkway we can return Helen and Dan's waffle iron." Because why? Because they *enjoyed* being put down and deftly recovering the upper hand from out of left field? And every time one of them did it Rudy was somehow involved, as little sense as that made; his most common response when corrected was to laugh, actually, which she had always admired.

To be fair, the reason everything annoying stuck to him was probably just that he was her much older and only brother and growing up she'd put in a lot more time with him than with her dad, who'd worked second and third shift for years. But why not the good stuff as well then? He had lovely table manners, for one thing, something their mother had been very big on; she had struggled with it but Rudy had developed a genuine enthusiasm, to the point at which she had more than once overheard them discussing—not disputing, no, but rather intently analyzing—the merits of an opinion they'd read in an Amy Vanderbilt column. Yet when some man she happened to be dining with had good manners, did she think of Rudy? No, she did not. At least not until much later. Why was that?

To be equally honest, perhaps even more so, some of the face-punching thing (not all, but some) was the result of so much time spent in the house with her husband, so many days without talking to a soul other than him. That is, she suspected that if she did punch Rudy it might helpfully reduce the stress she had built up over all these months from trying not to scream at, *preventing herself* from screaming at, never getting a single halfway decent chance to scream at Tom. Who (to be fair, but not too fair) couldn't really be considered at fault, at least not any more than anyone would be after suddenly going from a mostly weekend relationship with his wife to constantly negotiating her presence, but the question of fault didn't enter one bit into how much she needed to scream at him, which was *a lot*. More than she would ever have believed possible.

And the peculiar thing was, the more she pondered how lucky they were (before her mother got sick, anyway), the more she wanted to scream. The more she recalled how considerate of and generous to each other they had mostly managed to be over nearly 15 years, the more she wanted to scream. The more she reflected contentedly on her kids, in particular on how, while they weren't as close as she might have assumed they would be 20 years earlier (in fact she suspected they were just as glad they couldn't come over, or she go to them), they definitely liked her and Tom and felt quite happy to have them as mother and stepfather and maybe it was just that she was constitutionally incapable of appreciating the difference between relating to a child and relating to an adult, even if they did come from her womb—well, that was probably the most scream-provoking of all. Well no, it wasn't. Not the least bit fair really, but she knew that when her generally thoughtful husband did something *especially* thoughtful, when he went out of his way to figure out how he might manage to be thoughtful despite day after day of the two of them saying and doing the same damn things over and over, *that* was when she really wanted to go to town with the screaming. So sue her if it felt like punching her brother might help. She badly needed the relief.

While it truly was peculiar it was not surprising, not entirely. Because along with the scream quest, or maybe part of its cause—

definitely, absolutely part of its cause — was the queer sensation, beginning with the first lockdown, of ever-growing uncertainty about both how she should behave and what Tom might say or do. After all those years of well-established relations. Talk about disorienting. She'd had no idea whether he was feeling the same; he certainly hadn't shown it, but Mister Equanimity never showed he was disturbed by *anything*. (On being told a couple years before, for example, that her daughter, of whom he was very fond, had after an entire twenty-one year lifetime of utterly conformant and lawful behavior needed bail posted late one Saturday night, he'd simply inquired as to the charge, then with the same tranquility asked, "Would you like me to go with you? Or not?")

In any case, his internal experience had been neither here nor there, likewise her lack of a clue as to whether her own was caused by anything he was doing. She'd reviewed his actions and in fairness found nothing. But she'd been less and less interested in being fair, to tell the truth, and more and more in determining whether, in fact, as it had suddenly appeared, she knew him not nearly as well as she'd thought. He could probably handle that kind of doubt — who was she kidding, he could do it on his head — but for her it was way too destabilizing to tolerate for long.

Which must have been why she'd gone, late in April, when everything was still strange and unsettling — the empty roads, the carefully spaced lines outside markets, the masks, being disappointed all over again every time she recalled that they couldn't ask Ann and Lincoln to dinner — into his former "study" that was now his "office" (the difference being that before it was sort of her room too but now it definitely wasn't) to look for a pen, just after he'd announced that he badly needed rocky road ice cream and was going to go find some no matter how many lines he had to wait in and how long it took, and impulsively touched his mouse, noting to her surprise that his computer was not yet locked. (To be absolutely accurate, standing just outside the door it had passed through her mind that there had probably been time for it to lock, if he hadn't locked it himself before going to the hall to put on the leather jacket he still told her on a monthly basis he was so pleased to have received as a gift from her two years ago, which was probably her right brain's way of telling her left brain *it could still be unlocked*.) What if he were to suddenly come back in, she asked herself, to get his phone, for example, which she could see on his desk, and discover, even if she got out in time, that it was still unlocked? Would he suspect her? Would he be upset if he did? This had led her somehow to the conclusion that she was best off having a bit of a look around ("going through his phone" was what the young people called it in the advice columns, or the "agony columns" as her mother would have said) since he really wanted that ice cream and she would certainly have the place to herself for a while, which would happen again who knew when, and then locking it after.

And why should she "go through his computer"? Why not? People did it all the time, apparently. And it had indeed become clear that there was information she didn't have, blank spots that had been far less visible when he was at the office for fifty hours or more most weeks. Which had been pretty much all of their marriage. She loved him, she respected him, she appreciated him. But did she *know* him?

In terms of this immediate opportunity to find out (*serendipity*, she thought, remembering Miss Brown writing it on the chalkboard in the third grade) she didn't see much to look into unless she started opening files, which she was sure she could not manage without leaving incriminating traces, so when she spotted the Teams icon on the taskbar she went for that. The whole planet was using Zoom every day and twice on Sundays (as her mother would also have said) but at his office they had already been using Teams for meetings and chats and posting links and the like for some time, so when remotarama hit they were ready to go. Pausing before she clicked she'd called to mind, with pleasure (OK, marginally ungenerous pleasure) the time way last summer when Tom had attended a meeting on the patio in a tank top and one of his colleagues had messaged him **pushing the dress code there T**. This to a man who never went to the office in clothes he hadn't spent a lot of money on after much consideration. "What'd you answer?" she'd asked, when he told her at dinner. "I believe it was *huh*," he'd said. "And then *okay*. And then I turned off the video." As if the incident had not affected him in the slightest.

Well, that was it. To get to the point then, honestly, in all fairness, to the one true point, as a person who was indeed very much affected by things, by almost everything all the time, what had emerged as the culmination, the fulfilment of all her uncertainty was that it was Tom—her husband Tom, of all people—*Tom* who out of nowhere had said, "You might have been more careful." Just like that. And at the worst possible moment, when she could still have regained her balance, maybe, and been able to accept that exposing her mother had not been in some way deliberate, that no one could ever be sure how she became infected, a moment at which she might have had a prayer of remaining a woman who did not want to scream and punch people in the face. As if she didn't know—*as if she didn't know*—that she'd done something egregiously stupid in going anywhere near the shopping district. As if he didn't understand that when this woman who's been your mother for fifty-one years really wants something, is insisting, a woman who five years after her husband's passing is utterly uninterested in anything going on in the world outside her house, even a pandemic like the one her own father watched take his older brother, it is not so easy to keep saying no, to physically restrain an eighty-four year old in public when in the middle of you repeating "Ma, you have to stay in the car" for the seventh consecutive time she suddenly gets out with astonishing quickness and dashes for Seybold Shoes and you'd have to tackle her to the asphalt to stop her. As if she somehow knew the store would be crowded—against the rules!—and that Mary Louise Stewart would be just inside the back door and would of course throw her arms around her old friend, endlessly, while a bunch of people (some unmasked) pushed past, that she would be standing by, humiliated, trying to drag her mother out of there as if she were still a tired, complaining seven year old for another quarter hour. What a nightmare. And he thought she was being, what, sloppy? Negligent? *Inattentive?*

But at the time of the Teams incursion she'd still been mostly just curious (and only very slightly desperate). She had no interest in his calendar, which came up first, so after evaluating the options (and reminding herself to return to the calendar when finished!) she'd clicked Chat. Scanning down the list of his co-conversationalists she'd noticed Gabie Garcia, whom he'd told her about: a young woman with a builder husband and infant daughter who'd seemed nice enough although grim and overly contained after she'd started late last year but then on Teams, when they were sent home, had seemingly blossomed overnight, smiling and laughing often, and become one of his preferred colleagues to remote with. (To be refreshingly direct, she was bitterly envious of Tom for being able to remote with colleagues all the time—she could hear them laughing it up even with the "office" door closed—in fact at all, because the home version of her job, in which she was pretty much sufficient unto herself to begin with, had been utterly stripped of even the limited personal interactions she'd had at the office and was now almost a monk-in-his-cell type of thing. *Her* cell.)

Reflexively she bypassed Gabie ("not Gabbie?" "no, Gabie")—
whose photo did indeed look "contained", prim she would say—
and scrolled down to Jonathan, the group's "Shakespeare
scholar", whom she'd met a number of times at the company's
lavish (did "lavish" already incorporate excess in its definition? if
not she would say "overly lavish" or even "appallingly lavish")
holiday parties. She took a breath and clicked, began to scroll, and
almost immediately read

> Suppose a young analyst was hired, and one of the veteran
> team members felt that while this new person seemed nice
> enough, they projected a presence that if not actually severe
> was at least brisk and unemotive. Then suppose a killer virus
> hit and the veteran was surprised to find that the new person,
> who had seemed never to smile at the office, smiled all the
> time during the daily group video conferences, and that
> furthermore their smile was stunning and made them totally
> adorable. Good starting point for a netflix series, yeah?

OK, it was her husband who had written this. Teams (what a
moronic name) left no room for doubt on that score.

Jonathan had immediately (she checked the timestamp)
volunteered his own even less interesting screenplay proposal—
had he not understood that Tom had been talking about himself
and this "Gabie", lightly disguising it to stay clear of the
harassment policy, or had it been his way of brushing off any
discussion of his colleague's embarrassing pseudoadolescent
crush?—and then it got onto work matters. So after a moment's
hesitation she'd gone back to Gabie Garcia. And right away,
without any scrolling whatsoever, was confronted with

> I loved what you said at the meeting today. I think it's brilliant
> the way you can straighten out a discussion that's gone wrong
> while you keep everyone laughing or listening to your little

stories so they don't even see what you're doing. You're very good at your work, you know?

Thank you so much. Coming from you it means a great deal.

And there was a heart reaction on each comment. And she didn't need to hover the stupid pointer to know that the one on the first comment was Tom's and the one on the second was Gabie's. Reciprocating hearts.

Little stories? Little fucking *stories*? The fuck was this?

And how was a person supposed to feel about their spouse exchanging heart emojis with a much younger married member of the opposite sex they had been working with only a couple of months before a crisis so cruelly tore them apart?

Then she'd remembered, while staring at their pathetic little hearts (with 1s next to them, like there could be more than that between two people!) and trying to count the blank spots that had just been filled in, a story Tom had told about her, this Gabie, back in January (aka the carefree days). An hour or so into a particularly lame training the trainer had asked for an example of being stubborn, to which Gabie had raised her hand and offered, "Insisting on putting your loose change into those old-style paper rolls and bringing them to the bank instead of just using the machine at the supermarket." At the break Tom had approached her, not having spoken to her since they were first introduced, and smilingly remarked, "You were talking about your partner, I assume?", immediately regretting it because making assumptions was de facto inappropriate (especially with someone he suspected of being "grim"), but the woman had simply looked into the distance and replied, "Actually, I'm the stubborn one."

And now, much later, months later, many long dreary dismaying pandemic months that sometimes had her fantasizing about jumping off bridges later, she found herself repeatedly

remembering her failed *serendipity*, her search that had led to
nothing worth leading to, and wishing that for once in her life *she*
could be the stubborn one, not the patsy, the weakling, the
bullshitted, that she could be as honest as she had to with
everybody, all of them, leaving no room for doubt: she was not a
denier. That was not why it happened. She was very well
informed, she knew exactly what this fucking thing was, allowing
her own elderly mother to be infected had not been some sort of
statement. Yes she had been skeptical, she had been somewhat
casual at first, it was true she had been horrified when they
started shutting things down but she can't have been alone! And
very quickly she had become, unlike many others, fully capable of
appreciating all the grief they would soon be facing, not some but
all: people sick, people dying, hospitals and funeral homes in
chaos, frantic workers and businesses, millions of children
deprived of all normality in daily life until who knew when, the
safe and rich (like her and Tom) getting safer and richer while
everyone else took a dive. By now those were facts, not opinions.
But you could have opinions about facts. And between the facts
and your opinions and trying to understand all the conflicting
advice and people wanting what they wanted, COVID or no, plus
the fucking unexpected, it would take a superhero not to screw
up. Her mother if she were still around, her father, even her nutsy
uncles would go along with that proposition. Anyone could
understand it if they were trying. Only Rudy would make
something of it, god damn him.

And when she was calmer—and sometimes she *was* calmer,
that was when she could weep and miss the Ma who read to her
and played games with her and dressed her so beautifully for her
junior prom instead of the one who'd fled from her like an
escaping captive, desperate to get away—she knew enough to
know it didn't matter. Old people had died, thousands and

thousands of them, whole nursing homes full, and many more would die before they were rescued from this curse and even then they would keep dying because that's what people did. Her brother was right, she knew then; if it wasn't one thing it was another, so long as you died. More than once she remembered what her mother had whispered to her, gripping her hand so tightly, as the dirt was shoveled in on what had recently been her father: "I've been trying to prepare for this since the day I met him. And it didn't help at all."

It really wasn't a big deal; she was convinced of that too now. What with the line being so easy to cross.

And from that day to the present, from rocky road day, as she with some satisfaction thought of it, through the latest trip to the grocery to drift aimlessly among the other masked ghosts, despite opportunities too numerous to list, she had never, *never* given a moment's consideration to either so much as touching his fucking computer ever again or talking about, asking about, acknowledging the very existence of any Gabie Garcia. Nor had she ever felt the least bit inclined to be fair, honest, accurate, or direct about the matter, or any of its components.

Flight

The most remarkable thing, maybe, was her three-legged dog. Not that he'd never known any three-legged dogs before. Stella was also deaf and elderly; he'd known dogs like that too. But what he noticed from the first was how she would stand there looking instead of sniffing around and so on. Just looking. When he held out his hand she would study him for a few seconds and then come to him for petting. He had a persistent feeling that she'd always been like this, since before losing her leg, since long before growing old.

Then again, Abi was remarkably tall—his son, who to the amazement of all had reached six foot four and a half by his nineteenth birthday, was in the ninety-ninth percentile by his own report, well past it in fact, so given she was almost as tall there couldn't have been many like her—but it wasn't her stature that was striking, it was the way she carried it. Every time he saw her he was surprised all over again. She was without doubt very tall but nothing about her reflected this. As if she had grown up just middling and had suddenly been transformed—body, outfits, past photographs all rescaled—without ever being aware of it. As if she didn't care.

In high school she'd been a field hockey star and national science fair medal winner; shortly after graduating she'd gotten engaged to her best friend's older brother, who'd earned his Navy commission through NROTC and been accepted for flight training. She'd enrolled in community college while he went back to Pensacola. Around the time she would have been choosing courses for her fourth and final semester, five months before the wedding, her fiancé's plane had crashed with no cause ever confirmed. (Her linkedin page took him to the scholarship fund's website, which gave him many of these details, and he'd naturally googled the rest.) She'd soon enlisted in the Navy herself, spending most of her eight years on the reactor crew of a carrier. Now she was a twenty-eight year old senior in electrical engineering at the technical institute; she'd said she hoped to add a degree in cognitive sciences, but not to what end.

She'd appeared one day in late September after he and his wife had more or less given up on finding a tenant until the new year, when conditions might have eased enough for the nearby universities to bring back the graduate students, the pool of renters they'd been counting on when they bought the small downstairs apartment from their longtime neighbor after her retirement to Staunton, Virginia. Out of the blue she'd texted "can i come look this afternoon" then "sorry i mean the apartment, i'm abi". She'd taken it on the spot and seemed relieved to have done so. He gathered the campus housing she'd been offered had been in some way unacceptable and with the low-density residential scheme leaving nothing else available she'd been forced to live with her mother in her childhood home more than an hour's drive away. Completely plausible, just one more mundane pandemic story actually, but he'd nonetheless had the passing but oddly firm impression that she was really looking for somewhere to hide and liked the apartment above all because the entrance was twenty-five yards from the street and couldn't be seen until you got close.

She'd moved in so quickly and they'd been so pleased to be getting rent (although he regretted his haste in cutting it so dramatically, she clearly would have paid more) that he hadn't given it any further thought in the moment. But over time, as he got to know and like her, he'd come to intuitively empathize with her passion (as he perceived it) for a place of her own. Which also, yes, was a place to hide, if you were honest. Remembering their first meeting a month or so later he wondered if it was her mask that had made her seem fugitive. Not that it should have meant anything at all after more than half a year but though you thought you'd gotten used to them along with everything else in truth you never did. Just as every day still produced an "Oh yes the virus" moment. Not that masks were all bad. He loved the beauty they granted virtually everyone; as he'd learned with the Slovakian dental hygienist he'd had a crush on for a couple of years, when you couldn't see anything else the eyes—which were always lovely and vulnerable, and more often than not curious—stood for the face and so became the path for all that usually came to you through a person's idiosyncratic and opaque other features, filtering every bit of it for the better. For the first few months he'd hated the fact that no one could see his smile, which he was absurdly reliant on in dealing with strangers, until it occurred to him that the mask probably helped him in just the same way, that the authenticity and depth his artless eyes naturally provided might even be an improvement over his rote disarming gambit, which no matter how open he tried to feel and be was almost always at bottom a feint, like the hidden ball trick, and thus disarmed no one who mattered.

On the other hand a mask was a mask; you didn't spend sixty years understanding it as a means of hiding identity without becoming reflexively anxious when you saw one, at least to a degree. Even with the occasional masks he'd been spotting around town among the international students the past decade or so he'd been unprepared, OK maybe unwilling, to acknowledge them as primarily a science-based way of protecting yourself and your associates. Hiding your identity or conveying your fear of others, that's what mask-wearing had been. And still was, beneath his acquired (enforced) acceptance. He realized it was ridiculous to hold masks against people when everyone around him was wearing one for good reason but was glad to be aware of any and all misjudgments he was intuitively passing.

At any rate, once he'd had a few good looks at her unmasked face (the previous tenant, Tiffany, had always, *always* worn hers when she left the apartment after the lockdown started, even just to watch Champ, her own dog, sniff around the yard choosing a place to pee, and he hadn't even understood how tense this made him until she and her dachshund were gone) he decided that Abi was almost certainly not on the lam in any significant sense. Also that he wasn't the slightest bit attracted to her, which surprised him because she was young, vigorous, objectively pretty and quite likable, and even more so because he was typically attracted to any young woman with a pulse, never mind one he often bumped into, sometimes unexpectedly, as he wandered his own property. And she had a quirky but almost explosive smile. His lack of interest (of that kind, anyway) certainly wasn't due to her height—his wife had three inches on him—or anything else he could identify. He wondered if he was at long last starting to feel some restraint in contemplation of women roughly his daughters' ages, which seemed a fairly pathetic change to go through a decade and a half after the first had hit puberty. He was surprised that he was surprised when Rodeisha, his contractor friend, at the end of her first day working on the long-delayed reconstruction of the patio a couple of weeks after Abi arrived, texted **if you told me you had a cute tenant I would have dressed better**. Maybe he was just less interested overall, a somewhat shocking proposition but not unreasonable at sixty-three.

There was another newfound habit that weighed on him, as they suddenly all seemed to do, through his consideration of their new neighbor: life was so pared down, so narrowed, that the significance of every detail that remained was magnified, sometimes absurdly so. Take the grocery; it was his only regular very public outing so his impressions of, his interactions with the staff and the other shoppers and the people walking by in the lot as he parked the car or his bike and prepared his reusable bags had assumed an almost crushing importance. As if they would at some point gather to draft their report. Likewise, he seemed to be focusing on Abi with an intensity and frequency that was well out of proportion by any normal standard—wondering what he'd failed to tell her, if the place was maybe too small or otherwise disappointing, whether the water bill would go back down now because while she couldn't possibly be as laundry-focused as her predecessor she wore half again as much fabric as the petite Tiffany on any given day. Well *nothing* was normal as everyone he knew repetitively, obsessively, boringly reminded each other twenty-four/seven, why should he worry if *he* wasn't? They were both more or less trapped in the house for lack of anywhere else to go—his wife was at work every weekday, their remote college student son was often at his girlfriend's parents' home, and Abi's boyfriend Douglas seemed always to come to her—and she was so quickly at ease and so unaffectedly accepting, he came to understand, of the presence of others generally and his own in particular that before he knew it she'd transitioned from stranger to friendly acquaintance to a sort of probationary member of his household. Which caused him to want to look after her. Their eldest daughter, when he'd explained to her in an online chat how upset he was by Tiffany's sudden distance following their extended (and in fact totally uncalled for) drama concerning a limited mildew problem, which he'd come to see was actually mostly about her frustration and distress over how the virus had totally overthrown her plans, had written after a long pause, "A tenant's relationship with their landlord is mostly about power." Which had bugged him a lot for a couple of days. First of all, what relationship wasn't? And the power thing went both ways. And also, yes, of course he understood "don't make friends with the tenant" but that was who he was! That was how he did things. And Tiffany had happily accepted his many small but considerate gestures. Hadn't he immediately offered their own car, on literally the day after they'd first laid eyes on her, when she and her father—her parents had driven all the way from Highland Park to help her move in—needed to run an urgent errand and her mother and sister were off somewhere touristing and would not be back in time? When she told him that Champ had discovered he could get under the front gate by wriggling on his belly, hadn't he fitted one-by-twos (painted to match!) to the bottom within forty-eight hours, that very weekend? Hadn't they readily extended her lease through August for her convenience? Bottom line: whereas he'd told everyone how pleased they were about Tiffany for the first ten months of her tenancy only to be unreasonably (but quite painfully) burdened by her withdrawal for four more, he recognized after a month that their relationship with Abi—whatever it was or might become—would be the real thing, not a house of cards.

His wife tended to leave most interactions with others to him; she was generally less than confident with people she didn't know well and despite having arrived from overseas almost three decades prior still felt awkward about her accent (which was actually rather appealing) and the quality of her English (which was excellent, she was very articulate). But he soon saw that she too had been drawn out by the new arrival. He was astonished a week after Abi moved in to find them talking about gardening on the walkway. And by her suggestion a few days later that they give their tenant a slice of the coffee cake he'd just baked. "And for Douglas?" he'd asked. "Don't know if he's around." "Of course for Douglas" she'd replied with that spousal I'm-almost-hiding-my-derision-because-I-love-you lilt. In the event the act of knocking on her front door with plate in hand had been totally beyond him so after thinking it over he'd left the cake on the dryer in the laundry room, the neutral zone between their space and hers, and texted her it was there.

He wasn't obsessed. A day or two could easily pass with no thought of her. But how was he to drop it when her car was usually parked behind or in front of theirs and an ever-changing set of only vaguely identifiable objects was always piled intriguingly by her door, when he had to watch his step and stash poop bags around the yard because she wasn't managing to collect everything Stella left when let out to wander on her own so Abi wouldn't have to interrupt her coding or reactor designing or whatever it was she was doing in the apartment's bedroom which she'd made into a study by putting her bed where Tiffany's famous slightly mildewed couch had been because "I need elbow room to do schoolwork"? (He could not shake what she'd said when he'd apologized for the noise of the old patio being demolished: "I've done a lot of studying under ladderwells and jets taking off so you'll need more than that to rattle me.") When he mentioned the poop thing and after a week found it happening again he was absolutely not the slightest bit tempted to be judgmental, resentful, even annoyed; he actually found himself thinking "after all she's got a lot on her mind" when after all he did too. Didn't he?

In normal times they would certainly have invited her (or her and Douglas) for dinner and there really was no reason not to—the two of them were tested frequently by the school (Douglas was getting a doctorate in computational fluid dynamics but was also an RA in an undergraduate dorm, which was why they lived apart), he and his son were quite careful and limited in their movements, and while his wife went to work at the dental practice she was probably better protected there than anyone— except that his son had become very brittle about certain things, including letting anyone other than his girlfriend and sisters and the second sister's boyfriend into the house for more than five minutes, and he didn't want to rock that boat (not after the first time, anyway). And for all he knew Abi would feel the same and be put unpleasantly on the spot ("a tenant's relationship with her landlord is mostly about power"). One day he was musing on this while riding his bike and realized that a lot of the gloom and distress people were feeling resulted from being angry about what they couldn't do, were kept apart from, without having anyone to blame for it. "We're all simply trying to cope." Which were about the truest words he'd ever spoken (well, thought) in his life. The only people you could fault were the ones (mostly elsewhere, he read about but never saw them) who were flouting the rules and risking unnecessary death in order to do exactly the things he could not, but faulting them was not helpful in the least. Faulting someone else for your own envy and mixed feelings was unrewarding at best.

A related insight that came to him during a different ride not long after was the possibility that the anchor of his interest in Abi, so to speak, was his certainty that she wasn't laughing at him. He didn't know how he knew but he knew. Somewhere around nine or ten he'd started suspecting everyone around him who wasn't laughing to his face of either laughing behind his back or being capable of it, which made him feel so helpless and deterred (even an adult wouldn't know how to deal with something like that, never mind a ten year old) that his parents had taken him to be evaluated for depression. At first being depressed had seemed like an excellent defense against being laughed at but he'd soon come to his senses—obviously it would be exactly the opposite—and decided there was nothing for it but trying to cope. He did acquire in the process the beginning of a notion that everyone else was also trying to cope with some way they would rather (much rather) not be but for years, until well after college really, he'd had to invest so much energy in isolating and suppressing his inner humiliation that he'd had little to spare for the problems of others. Which he was in any case certain he could not qualify.

One afternoon as darkness fell, not long after the weather had turned seriously cold, he was standing by the trash and recycling bins behind the front stoop after cleaning out the dryer vent, about to haul them to the walkway to be filled with the household's weekly ejecta—just another trash day at number 157, which he estimated he'd experienced around fifteen hundred of since his maiden voyage more than thirty years earlier, one much like another except when some unusual item such as a hopelessly worn cat tree or a broken dehumidifier was being discarded and of course there were the maybe eight per year that were on Friday instead of Thursday on account of a holiday, often making it a challenge to fit in the extra day's production—when she silently approached with a large paper bag, startling him.

"Hey," she said in her I'm-not-laughing-at-you way, "didn't mean to make you jump."

"Jumping's good for us old guys," he said, immediately regretting it. "What have you got there?"

"I was wondering, what should I do with a broken mirror? The glass from it, I mean."

Though she was utterly unteasable he reflexively tried: "I don't want to get mixed up with someone who broke a mirror."

Again, *I'm not laughing at you*: "I think it's too late for that."

"I'll take it," he said, holding out his hand. "I'll put it in another bag and then in our trash."

But she held the broken glass to herself more closely, it seemed. "Haven't I had enough bad luck?"

He really had no response whatever, wish as he might that he did.

"I mean, I know you googled Jacen. Everybody does. That's why I put him on linkedin."

"I'm so sorry, Abi," he nearly whispered.

"For googling him?"

"No, that he –"

She waved him off. "That was cheap. I know what you meant."

He wanted to cry. She'd been only twenty.

"Anyway now *Douglas* needs a *break*, I'm told. That's why I dropped the mirror. Let the bad luck fall on him."

"You don't need him." Still whispering.

"You think I don't know that?" she said almost bravely, almost fiercely but somehow still matter of fact despite the darkness, still Abi despite the waiting bins, despite the keen strangeness of their having this conversation, despite Jacen's jet spinning down into the ocean, and he understood all of a moment: it was not she who was in flight.

Year One

Get back, get back, get back to where you once belonged
Get back, get back, get back to where you once belonged
Get back Jo!

— "Get Back", Lennon & McCartney, 1970

The Druggist

Her schedule says **9.30** so she is there at 9.00. Because that's the way she is. They laugh at the store when she arrives for a 2 o'clock shift at 1.25. They laughed in high school over how she was always first to show at debate team, chorus, gay-straight alliance. But she has long been clear that she would rather be amusing than annoying, which is what being late makes you.

She sits in the empty chair by the facility administrator's closed door, wishing she'd thought it through before showing the front desk guy her ID and reminding him who she was because she'd much rather wait in her car. But there's no way she's going back and explaining this to him. So she pulls out her tablet and takes up a novel she finds only so-so and is considering giving up on. When the administrator arrives a few pages later she immediately stands.

"I'm sorry, Ms. Malhotra—I hope you haven't been waiting long?"

"It's my own fault, I came ridiculously early."

The woman laughs. She's a very pleasant-looking person with a wide face, dark skin, and short, very natural hair. The badge on her jacket says Norma Moseby, LICSW, RN. "You know, I often do the same. But I'm usually not so willing to admit it."

"I guess I'm compulsively honest," says Roshni. Norma Moseby looks at her as if it's kind of an odd remark, which she supposes it is, then laughs again.

"At any rate," she says, "I think we have a few minutes before it's time to head to the vaccination area, so please come in and sit down."

"You have a vaccination area?"

"Actually, it's the *smoking* terrace, I'm embarrassed to say. Today it's for vaccinations."

"It must be quite a job to convince forty or fifty-year smokers to even consider quitting," Roshni says, taking the large envelope labeled PINE MANOR from her bag.

"You can't imagine," says the administrator. "Or maybe you can."

"Well, I see the ones who are at least trying to stop. When they come for their gum and patches and so forth."

The woman sighs and looks at the big clock. "Now, Ms. Malhotra—"

"Please call me Roshni."

"Yes of course, Roshni. I'm Norma." Roshni can't help glancing at Norma's badge, but only for a moment. "What we have for you today is very simple. We've interviewed them and gotten their consent forms, we've assigned them all time slots—all you have to do is say 'Next!' and give them their shot. And their card—we've filled in your pharmacy's name—with the lot sticker. One of our staff will add the other information."

"Actually, I'd like to verify the consent form for each recipient, and briefly review the questionnaire."

"But there's no need—"

"It's a matter of professional responsibility, Norma. I'm sure you understand."

Norma thinks for a moment.

"Yes, I do. That's fine."

"And I'd prefer to fill out the card myself."

"Roshni, all this will add considerable time—"

"Yes, I know. There are fifty-four residents and twenty-two staff on the list."

"Which means if you add even two minutes for each you will extend the process and your visit by two and a half hours. And be far behind the appointment schedule in the later stages."

"Well, yes. I see what you mean." She still doesn't quite have the knack of talking to older figures of authority, but she's learning. "How about this? I can check the consent forms very quickly. And I'll enter only the name of the recipient on the card. Just so it can't be misused."

Until this point the administrator has looked vexed, but now she smiles behind her mask. "Well, you are meticulous. And conscientious. Which is exactly what we want in our pharmacists, isn't it?"

It's difficult, but she allows herself to smile back. Although in her case it probably isn't visible at all.

"I just have two questions, Norma. Have any of the recipients had their first shot already? Have any been infected in the past?"

"No and no. And we last tested everyone four days ago."

"Oh, that's excellent. Thank you."

"Ought to have the hang of it by now. We were one of the first facilities in the state to get serious about this and we've kept very strict policies in place for nearly a year." She sighs again. "Maybe after today we can think about relaxing a little."

"I'm sure it's been a very long year for you," says Roshni. "For all of you."

"And we did lose five residents at the beginning. Almost before we understood what was happening."

"That must have been very hard."

"Ms. Malhotra," says Norma, getting to her feet, "you really can't imagine."

She is set up at the center of the smoking terrace, one wall of which is several large sliding doors that can be opened to various degrees for air, weather permitting. The residents, about a dozen so far, are sitting in distanced folding chairs and wheelchairs at the end to her right. At the other end is a small table; the staffer sitting there, presumably to fill out the cards, waves to her and she waves back. Out in the cold, icy garden she sees a not particularly old-looking man in a wheelchair, smoking. Rough on him, this repurposing.

Scanning the list, she is again annoyed that the staff come after the patients, rather than being mixed in, although she's not sure why; there are all sorts of plausible reasons for it. Well, she's certainly not going to mention it to the administrator. She has no desire whatever to be called on Jo's virtual carpet again to explain again why someone found fault with her.

Another staffer arrives with a cold case of vials. "Oh my," says Roshni. "That's not nearly enough."

"Other one's in the freezer," says the man—boy actually. Although broad shouldered and well muscled he is very young. "Figured I'd let it stay cold until we need it."

"Yes, of course, that's totally right. Thank you."

He squints down at her. "You a nurse?"

"Pharmacist."

"You don't look like a nurse. How come they didn't send one?"

She shrugs. "I was available. We're allowed by law to do this."

"Yeah, I know, get my flu shot at Walgreen's," he says as he walks away. She can barely hear him mutter "Allowed by *law*, huh?" and chuckle before he crouches by one of the wheelchairs to talk with its occupant.

"All right," Roshni says, a little loudly, "let's get this show on the road." This is one of her father's beloved American expressions; he almost never says them to any actual Americans except his children and nephews but they make him feel more at home. She reaches under the table for the syringe and needle boxes and puts them to the right of her chair, and then the sharps bin to her left. The pile of consent forms, the list, the deck of vax cards, the vials, and the sheet of lot stickers are in front of her. She checks the number on the stickers against the number on the vials and of course they match.

Picking up the first consent form and glancing at the clock, which says 9.55, she calls "Mrs. Rivera? Anita Rivera?" and pulls out a syringe.

Of the twenty-one she has done so far, five have been in tears to some degree. Four of the women and one man. Tears of relief, she imagines, and gratitude and bitterness; there are so many reasons for them to weep. When Jo gave her the assignment and asked if she minded, Roshni had to stifle a laugh. Of course she doesn't mind.

"Mr. Wiley? Benjamin Wiley?"

She glances at her phone lying in front of her. More or less on schedule. Norma has no cause for complaint. So far.

The man approaching her table is bent but still tall; he must have been a giant in his prime. He stops by the chair, scowling, and she braces herself for trouble.

"Won't you have a seat, Mr. Wiley?"

111

He stands looking at her for another couple of seconds, then carefully sits down.

"Sorry," he says. "I'm anxious and confused about this thing."

"I'm sorry to hear it, sir."

She thinks that makes him smile, a little. His eyes certainly seem to soften.

"It's ridiculous, I've no reason to be."

"Personally, when I'm nervous, I try not to ask why. Better to focus on becoming calm instead."

"Oh, I know why. It's that fool of a son of mine, keeping after me about hoaxes and conspiracies."

"And yet here you are, getting the vaccine."

"Yeah," says the man, rolling up his sleeve.

"You know," she says as she swabs his skin, then uncaps a new vial and picks up the syringe she has ready, "these days it's often not so much foolishness as being badly misinformed."

"Oh, he's always been a fool."

"My father says that about me, sometimes," she tells him as she puts the needle in and presses the plunger, then carefully pulls it out, "but I know he's proud of me, and I'm betting you're proud of your son too." She holds up the needle to show him.

"Go ahead, I'm ready."

"It's done," she tells him, tossing the syringe in the bucket.

"You're kidding."

"No," she says as she applies the band-aid, "it's done." She puts a lot sticker and his name on the card, then picks it up and holds it out to him.

He carefully stands and takes the card. "Well, you're very good at this, miss. Thank you."

"You're very welcome, Mr. Wiley." He starts back to the chairs but the staffer at the far end calls out "Hey Ben! Over here!" and he rolls his eyes at Roshni before heading that way.

She can't help but notice that this next shot will be the thirty-eighth, meaning that at its conclusion she will be halfway through. Assuming they all show up and there are no last-minute extras. She wishes she didn't always notice these things but again, this is who she is and she accepts it. At least she has finally managed to stop resetting Trip Meter B every time she drives her Prius (Trip Meter A being used to track each tank of gas, which the Prius already does for her) so she can compare the total mileage to Google's figure when she gets to her destination.

The staffer who has been handling the chair pulls it away and a wheelchair glides in. The woman in the wheelchair, Jeanne Schmidt, looks strong and alert. Before Roshni can greet her she says, "My own daddy was a druggist." According to her form she turned ninety in July, which would explain why she uses that term. "With his own store. I was always proud of that. I would boast about it on the playground."

"It's nice that you were proud of him, Mrs. Schmidt. Do you mind if I push your sleeve up a little further?"

"Go ahead, dear. Frankly I'd have been proud of him if he worked in the sewers. But I did like to think about his giving medicine to people for their children—children like me, only sick, which I almost never was."

Swabbing the woman's upper arm, Roshni marvels at the texture of her skin. If you looked only at this small area, you wouldn't know if she was ninety or thirty-five.

"Of course that's what created such problems for him later."

113

She picks up the syringe she prepared and uncaps it, then takes the open vial in her other hand. "Oh?" She has just glanced into the needles box and is slightly alarmed by what she saw there.

"Yes, it almost caused my parents to divorce."

Although she is working through her concern about the needles—if her estimate is right she may have to stop using separate needles for the draw and the shot, which will make the shot more likely to hurt—she looks up. "I don't see how it could do that."

"That's because you didn't live during the Depression, dear. He started giving credit to people who couldn't pay for their prescriptions which usually meant, as he well knew, that he would never see the cash. I'm talking about established customers who had families but no money. Which was a great many of them in those days."

"That was very good of him," Roshni says, bringing the needle to the woman's arm. "Here comes the stick." She feels idiotic saying this, especially so many times in one day, but she hasn't come up with anything better.

"I agree," says Jeanne Schmidt as Roshni puts on the band-aid. "But my mother didn't like it one bit. Said his responsibility was to her and me and my brother. And in fact he eventually had to sell out to one of the chains, when I was eight."

"But you never went hungry?" Another one bites the sharps bucket. Now the card and the sticker, again.

"No," says Jeanne, looking at her the way Norma did, as if she's just said something odd. Which she supposes she has. "We were fine. But he was strictly an employee from then on. Never had his own business again."

114

"What's the holdup?" calls a man with a walker. "It's vaccines, ladies, not book group."

"Completely forgot to mention," says Norma. "We scheduled in a thirty-minute lunch break for you."

"Thank you," says Roshni, gratefully removing her latex gloves. "But I don't need that long."

Norma smiles. "Suit yourself," she says. "Pick it up whenever you're ready. We're behind anyway. Did you bring something to eat?"

"I did."

"Because we actually have halfway decent food here and they've started serving lunch, I can get you some."

"I have my lunch right here," she says touching her bag under the table. "But thank you."

"You bet."

As Norma walks away Roshni glances at the waiting area. There are four residents sitting there and one of them is Jeanne Schmidt. Although it has just occurred to her how nice it would be to find a place to sit alone for a few minutes, she reaches into her bag for her lunch sack and thermos, gets up, and takes a seat near Jeanne instead. They're a good seven feet apart until she stands and moves her chair to half that. The woman was tested four days ago, after all.

"I was very much hoping to talk more with you," says Jeanne.

"Yes," says Roshni. "I was interested by what you said."

"About my father?"

"Yes," she says after chewing and swallowing a mouthful of food. "Was he an immigrant?"

"His parents were."

"It's a struggle immigrants go through. Doing well is so important. But you have to be who you are."

"Yes. That's well put. It's not that my mother wasn't reasonably kind. Or that my father didn't want to get ahead. But he could never resist people in need, and to her success was everything."

Roshni has been hurriedly eating while listening to Jeanne. She had no idea she was so hungry. As she takes another forkful a staffer in flowered scrubs approaches. "This is the place for the shot, right?"

"Yes, it is. I'll be starting again soon, after I finish my lunch."

"Oh, my appointment isn't for a while yet. Just wanted to be sure I had the right place."

"You have the right place, Cheryl," says Jeanne. Cheryl waves at them and calls "Thanks!" as she walks away.

"And about pharmacy," Roshni goes on. "You know, most of us go into it because it pays well and jobs are easy to find. But also because it's meaningful. Giving, as you say, medicine to children. To everybody."

"Yes, my father had purpose. That's so important."

"It is, but from my point of view so is control. And it's different these days. For every customer who clearly appreciates us, there's one with a problem." Another bite; Jeanne is very patient. "It's too soon to refill or the insurance insists on generic or we're out of stock and they have no way to get to the other store. Or worst of all they have no insurance and can't afford what they need."

"So people are stressed and upset."

"Well yes, exactly. Just last week a woman came in the day her prescription expired. And it turned out she'd actually ordered the refill a month before and then not picked it up despite the texts and emails and so forth, so eventually our assistant returned it to stock. It was something she really needed. She said, "Are you telling me that two weeks ago it was waiting and now I can't get it?" She was frantic. I explained everything six times: that our system knew the prescription was expired and I couldn't override it, that return to stock after two weeks is a very strict company policy, that I couldn't even give her two doses without an active prescription. She said 'I had a lot of trouble to deal with, that's why I didn't come' and I assured her I understood. I offered to call her doctor's office myself to see if I could get them to send a new prescription immediately." She can hear her mother saying, *What a long story you are telling!* "But she didn't want to listen. She just kept repeating 'Are you kidding me?' —except more profanely— with half a dozen other customers waiting and watching because Khuyen was at lunch and it was only me, until finally she left. Still frantic."

While Jeanne waits to see if her soliloquy is truly over, Roshni looks into her plastic container, but it's as she thought: there's nothing left.

"That doesn't sound like much fun, dear," says Jeanne. "But the system and the regulations aren't your fault or responsibility. And you're fulfilling your purpose even when it doesn't go smoothly."

Roshni is surprised a woman this smart doesn't get it. "I *wanted* to give her the medication even though the prescription had expired," she explains, "but I *couldn't*. That's what I mean by control. I felt terrible for her and wanted to help but couldn't. And will never be able to in such a situation."

"I guess that's true."

"I couldn't even call her doctor without her agreement, which for some reason she wouldn't give."

"Maybe because she preferred being frantic?"

This strikes Roshni as a very perceptive remark.

"Okay, you're right, it was her fault I couldn't help her. But still I couldn't. And that's why I think I agree with your mother."

"Oh? Really, dear?"

"Not about the money *per se*. Because he gave up control."

"I don't follow."

"Well, after all, he lost the ability to give prescriptions on credit when he lost his drugstore, didn't he? I so envy his freedom to make his own decisions, and he gave it up. Maybe if he'd done it for fewer families—only for the most serious illnesses, say—he could have avoided selling out and becoming like me. Restricted by someone else's rules."

Jeanne sits and looks thoughtful for a little while.

"You're so smart and insightful, you actually remind me of my father." She laughs. "He'd have been better off if he'd had you to advise him."

"Oh, don't be silly, Jeanne," Roshni says, warmly she hopes.

"You know, dear, when my father was young, pharmacy was an appealing profession for a lot of smart young Jewish men. The sons of immigrants. Of course it was best to become a doctor but that was so lengthy and expensive and you had to get past the quotas; being a druggist was a kind of compromise with reality. Now it seems to be the same sort of thing for young women like you. Well, I mean young nonwhite women with immigrant parents."

Roshni finds she cannot respond to this. She tries to think of a comment or observation but she's blank, perhaps because of the rapidly mounting feeling that she's already said way too much to someone she doesn't know. Jeanne waits an uncomfortably long time before speaking again.

"I'm sorry. You think that was a racist remark. And I suppose it was."

"No. I mean, I'm not offended. And it's true, every pharmacist at our store is a young Asian woman. Although one is a second generation American." This seems like a terribly dry and insincere answer. "But I guess I would say yes, it's probably best to avoid saying 'people like you' and making assumptions about immigrants and so forth. And the term now is *of color*, so *women of color*."

"Or maybe you're not too crazy about the comparison."

"What do you mean? What comparison?"

"Being compared to Jews, dear."

"Why would that bother me?"

"When I was growing up in Chicago in the thirties and forties there were many it would have bothered a great deal."

"Well you outlasted them, didn't you? And people are not so much that way anymore."

Jeanne looks at her for a couple of seconds. "Are you telling me you don't run into bigots? People who hate getting their prescriptions from an Indian?"

That's a topic she's certainly not going to discuss here and now. "Yes, of course. But that's a topic I'm not going to discuss here and now." She looks again into her container; it's still empty. Taking a last swig of tea from her thermos and standing, she says, "I'd better go use the restroom and get started again. It's been very nice talking with you, Jeanne."

"I enjoyed it," says Jeanne, starting to roll away. But then she stops and returns.

"Listen, dear—Roshni, isn't it?" she says, looking up at her. "I want to tell you something. I've been here since ten o'clock because I had nothing better to do. I've been watching you the whole time. I want you to know that I see how kind you are."

Roshni actually laughs a little. "Me?" she asks, pressing her open hand to her chest.

"Yes you. I know you think you're an organized and efficient person. A *prepared* person. And I'm sure you are. But I'm too old to care about that." Jeanne is speaking in a very focused, earnest way, as if saying something especially important. It's slightly frightening, but only slightly, and that probably because she's ninety. "What I see—what I like a great deal—is that you're kind and respectful and considerate. You've had a nice word for everyone and you've been very patient."

Roshni wonders if Jeanne could possibly mean it. She wants to look around to see if there's another pharmacist in the room.

"Well. If I've helped anyone get through this more easily, I'm glad."

Jeanne carefully wheels forward until she is close enough to take Roshni's right hand. With any other stranger, at any other time or place, she'd take it right back, but through the application of some talent she didn't remotely know she had she is able to calmly overcome a lifetime of certainty about what is and isn't allowed and let Jeanne have and hold it. Which reminds her how long it's been.

"Roshni, dear, it isn't *this*. It's not the vaccinations. It's *everything*. Really, we've been through so much bullshit, I'm sorry but that's the word, and so much sorrow. So much loss, so much lack of understanding. We're all worn out, the staff are worn out, we have so little left for each other. But you came today to do a wonderful thing, which by itself would have been more than enough, and you've been so *generous* about it. Generous. It's meant a lot to every single person, even if they don't know it."

Roshni shakes her head in a reflexive effort to clear it. But lack of clarity is not the problem.

"Even if *you* don't," says Jeanne, letting go of her hand. For which she is suddenly, unaccountably sorry.

They seem at an impasse. She should say something. *Just say thank you.* But she can't.

Jeanne stares up at her. "Don't change, dear. I mean it. Don't ever change. Keep on giving credit to the parents with no money. You're a mitzvah." Then she starts away again and this time, very rapidly for a ninety year old, crosses the terrace and disappears through an open door.

And instead of just as rapidly running out to her car and driving away, Roshni realizes, as she so badly wants to do, she's going to stand there in shock and tears, with people looking and more coming in by the moment, until it wears off, at least enough so she can manage to ask for the restroom and wash her face and then come back and do the remaining thirty-four vaccinations. Which she is inescapably obligated to complete. Whether she has enough needles or not.

The Boy Who Cried Pandemic

He is in their way. He is always in their way, even when they are at the supermarket or walking in the forest. Even in his dreams. Their dreams too, probably; they will never say so, but he knows what he knows.

Spring was easier. He had nowhere else to go and they all thought it would be just through the summer. Cheerful and making the best of it, which even at twenty he'd done plenty of already (like the breakup with Jenny) plus his parents wrote the book.

Eleven months later, the end still undefined, it's another matter entirely; it's him in charge of his own life, like they say they want. He got his first hint when he told them he thought campus in the fall would so totally suck he'd be nuts not to stay home and they instantly agreed. His father quoted, again, his favorite of the moment (by some guy in the Post, what a surprise) about how COVID campuses would resemble "a monastery combined with a minimum-security prison". Like his dad doesn't think he could use a little of both. Like his mom wouldn't rather—not that she is a prude—that he and Shireen do their fucking in their rooms at school and not down the hall from where she is lying, trying not to hear (which she can't, because they don't make any noise because they're not complete jerks, but still she tries).

Now he is starting his *second* intrusive semester and it's not like he doesn't have reason for discomfort. Such as having heard his dad tell a friend how they'd had "all of each other's attention" and could be "spontaneous for a change" — until he showed up and kicked them out of paradise. By not taking the monk/embezzler route, by giving up his claim in favor of some guy who couldn't possibly do "remote learning" jammed into a two-bedroom apartment with his mom and four siblings, by not making them sit down with him and talk it through. If they had all had it out at the point of decision it might be much better now, no matter where he ended up. But no. No questions, no discussion, just variations on "no problem".

He is fully aware that a jillion other students are enduring the same purgatory. Stress test. Whatever. But they are all on their own and cannot assist each other. He is keenly aware that there are a jillion worse troubles but not knowing what it's like to experience those he finds the fact of their existence unhelpful. He is painfully aware that his parents love him fiercely and could never be dissuaded, no matter what he did. He sees that at some level it's another version of living at home at twelve or seventeen. But this time he chose it! Everyone knows you can stand life with your parents only because you have to. And now when they look at him they are definitely thinking *he didn't have to*, even if they don't know it. And it's beyond freaking belief but they really seem not to.

They said it was "a good idea" when he first told them his thinking. His advisor also called it "a good idea". Shireen of course thought it was the sickest thing since forever; it turned out she'd already reached the same conclusion (though she preferred "utterly suck" over "totally") and was hoping he'd agree because that would be so much easier than having to break him down. Her house was about a mile from his parents' — they were high school classmates and he now understood that showing Jenny the door had at bottom been motivated by the way Shireen looked at him across the cafeteria from where she sat with her crew, singling him out of his crew, although they didn't actually happen until that summer when they met to talk about college and even then he had to work really hard to catch up to the idea that someone this smart, articulate, hot was as interested in him as she gave every sign of being—which meant that a) getting together for silent fucking would be almost as easy as at school and b) when she got tired of listening to her mother question their relationship (sometime during their first year, she'd told him, he'd been upgraded from "the white boy" to a faintly sarcastic "your special friend", although recently his actual name had come up a time or two) she could deal with it either by spending a couple nights in his room silently fucking him after dark for a change, then beaming (ironically? she wouldn't say) at his father's BLM shirts over breakfast, or bringing the white boy over there in person and laughing with him in her room about what her mother must be imagining them doing. (And then, of course, fucking him. This has been going on for more than two years now and he still feels he must be dreaming.)

So had *he* considered it a good idea? He must have, mustn't he? Certainly he was surprised it was so fuck-all simple to decide. Now it looks like the worst idea of his life—yes, he knows, the worst *so far*—although he is not sure why. Beyond his being always, *always* in their way.

That summer, with first year move-in about ten days away, they went for a long walk by the river to get real. Not that they called it that, they just knew. And while both were very clear, it turned out, on what they wanted real to include, i.e. steady companionship and some serious fucking, they didn't know yet, not for absolute sure, that it was mutual. And he, at least, had additional concerns, like wasn't it obvious that she'd soon consider him shallow? And weren't her friends laughing about him and did she laugh with them? And did she get that he was at least as psyched to discuss major issues and listen to her sing and go on bike trips as he was to fuck her brains out?

The experience was intensely awkward, no doubt, but they forced it anyway and in the end it was clear they were pretty much what his dad likes to call "on the same page".

And almost the most satisfying thing about it (almost!) was the way his mom and dad were rocked, practically staggered, when he first brought her home, as they 'd agreed was required on both sides before school started. (Neither wanted to be suddenly sending a bunch of texts in October to prepare their folks for a different Thanksgiving look.) He was eager for this, in part because they had already been at each other's houses when they were otherwise empty, which felt shitty and risked being ratted on by a neighbor, but mostly because he was jazzed to impress his parents and to get to know Amber, Shireen's mom.

He loved the look on his mother's face when he returned from walking Shir home. "Oh my god, dear, where did you *find* this girl?" Yes! She was excited. Guess I'm not a loser after all, Mom. Actually it did kind of fulfill most of what she'd always said about him, that he could interest a girl this lit. It was also the start of an ongoing suspicion that she couldn't help wishing, just a little, that he could be more like Shireen. In certain respects.

They have no idea, not the slightest notion of how anxious he is, absolutely none, no clue that he has no right or reason as a college junior to be this anxious about anything, never mind all the stuff in the future, years away, that is giving him fits. (As if the freaking virus and the stinking remote classes plus the climate and white supremacy and whether or not all cops are bastards isn't enough on his mind.) Shireen has some idea—she's very helpful, actually, she is much more mature than he is and beyond that he is sure she was born wise—but they have none. And he isn't about to give them one; his footprint in the household is big enough as it is, thank you. It would be a lot less of a problem (OK, fair, he would be much less anxious) if it were like high school, with him at soccer practice or out with his friends half the time, or last summer when he'd spent a crazy number of hours doing tour after tour and piling up an even crazier amount of tips, but that stuff is right out the window for him and the rest of creation. He goes nowhere except Shireen's house or for distanced runs with his old pal Hubens. And yeah, to pick up the takeout his parents order with amazing frequency "to help the local economy". (Not that it doesn't, but could they also just admit they love having takeout all the time?)

Anyway, anxious—he's lost track of what that even means, what it's for, what the stakes could possibly be to get him in such a state, so *of course* it's going to apply to his messing up this golden "empty nester" thing they had going for a whole year and a half.

"In case you think it's easy," Amber said as they stood in her kitchen, on first meeting, "I can tell you it's not." Suddenly it was only two days to move-in. Shireen was upstairs doing some damn thing and taking her sweet time about it.

"I'm sorry?"

"Turning your daughter over to someone else to look after." He started to panic because he thought she meant him, then got that she was talking about the college.

"No ma'am, I don't think that."

A very sharp look. "That *ma'am* for me? Or do you always talk that way?"

"Pretty much always. Close as I can come."

Her hand was resting motionless on the counter. "I thought it might be because we're black." He noted the plural pronoun and everything somehow flipped in an instant. Shireen's all she has, he thought. She's looking at hard time.

"Well, I feel better when I'm polite. So I have these habits, I guess, to sort of keep me on track."

"Takes more than that."

"Oh totally, ma'am. Way more."

An even sharper look, a little scary.

"If you prefer I not call you ma'am, I sure won't."

"I prefer you call me Amber." That surprised him. Shireen had specifically warned him not to use her first name. And she didn't sound like she preferred it at all.

"You're telling me you truly believe they don't know how much you're bothering them," says Shireen as they lie on her bed listening to her mother listen to early Dylan (she's insanely eclectic, next it might be Cardi B or Ravel or Tatum or something from Hair or Book of Mormon) as she washes up after dinner.

"Never said 'bothering'. I said in their way."

She rolls her eyes.

"It's different, Shir," he says, propping up on one elbow. "*In your way* isn't that you don't like it, just you want it someplace else. Also, it's not a 'how much', it's binary. I'm in their house, I'm in their way. I'm in the dorm, I'm not in their way."

"That's all as it may be, bae. To me it's only a word game."

"What's that supposed to mean?"

"Lemme ask you something, young man. If they haven't yet discovered you're 'in their way', doesn't that mean you're not? Aren't we talking about the *experience* of having someone in your way?"

He can't argue with that. Doesn't want to, really.

"Lemme ask you something else. What exactly is making you stressed — the part about being in their way or the part about their not admitting it?"

"There you go again. I never said I wanted them to *admit* anything."

"Well, you just about did, sugar," she says, snuggling up to him and sighing the way she does pretty much every time she snuggles up to him. As if touching him somehow makes her so damn happy. Like, half as happy as it makes him.

Now her mom is getting ready to walk the dog, who is barking like crazy because she sees the leash. We're creatures of habit, he thinks. The dog barks, Shireen sighs, I stress.

"I actually have one more question," she says around kissing his neck. "If you'll be so kind."

"Oh, I'm kind," he tells her, pushing her onto her back, getting between her legs and resting his head on her breasts. "I'm all kinds of kind."

"How much do *I* stress you?"

He raises up to look at her. "You're kidding."

"I wanna know."

"Not at all, baby," he says with conviction. "Never once since you first you looked at me with those incredible eyes peeking out from under that adorable do."

She chuckles. "Sweet talker, boy," she says, "but I'm not sure I believe you." He isn't sure either. Would she be lying so still and

131

relaxed, would she be chuckling if she didn't? Is it remotely possible she doesn't care?

"It's true," he says, very quietly. "I love that about you."

He can hear her heart. Her magic breasts are rising and falling beneath his cheek as she breathes, a bit heavily, he thinks, for lying motionless on a bed. It gets heavier as they lie there.

"Even more," she says at last, "than my being 'the greatest piece of ass in the history of the world' quote unquote?"

He is trying to figure out how she wants him to answer when he realizes she is laughing.

"My god, she's lovely."

The sun was very hot. The crowd was large and lively. Back in another lifetime, when crowds were not scary as shit, when you could just decide to have some fun in about any way you wanted and could pay for, his mother had actually come to the beach with them, baffling and pleasing them both. She and he were sitting on the blanket watching Shireen go past the restrooms, fifty yards away, and turn the corner to head for the snack stand.

"Yeah. I was just thinking that." He looked at her. She was grinning happily.

"Don't you feel crazy lucky?"

"Every fucking day, Mom." He was *so* glad he could say this to her. "Honestly. Every day."

"Don't you worry someone will try to take her away from you?"

He glanced at her again, on the verge of being offended until he saw she'd moved on to the teasing grin. He lay down on his stomach and rested his head on his crossed arms.

"You know," he said after a couple minutes, "if I worry about anything it's that she'll finally see through me."

To his astonishment she didn't reassure him. "You mean, decide you're not who she thought you were?"

"Right." He turned his face toward her.

"Sweetie, everyone worries about that. All the time."

"What? Do you mean it?"

She shrugged. "Well I certainly do. Not really all the time, but at least once in a while. Most days I feel your dad has always worshipped me and always will, on some I put the question out of my mind, and every so often I'm thinking he'll discover I'm a fraud."

"After thirty years? No shit?"

"No shit, Sherlock." This was the grin he liked best of all.

Something about it—the sun and her grins and maybe her coming out of nowhere with one of her Adult Observations, the way she used to—reminded him, with no detail but real power, of some similar moment on some beach long ago, in the days when all he cared about was his boogie board and sandcastles and getting ice cream and not bikinis and the girls wearing them, when afterwards they would shower or towel the sand off and drive to the seaside town they all liked so much, his father saying (as he did every time!) that he didn't mind paying a lot for parking on a day like today, in a place like this, with the people he loved, and walk to the penny candy store he especially liked (it had a real nickelodeon!) and the seafood takeout they especially liked (he always got a hot dog!) and then to the jetty to sit on the rocks together and eat and watch the boats go by and offer fries to the gulls, and he was sharply moved.

"Yo, Mister Privilege," said Shireen, throwing his Drumstick cone on the blanket by his head, "here's your slop. And here, ma'am," she went on as she presented, with a flourish, a jumbo

Chipwich to his mom, "is the *good* stuff. As promised."

It's not just him who's going nowhere. If he had a million bucks he would happily trade it for his father working at the office like before. For *one week* of that. His mother has been back at the clinic since it reopened in June; while she doesn't work full-time she goes there regularly. And he at least goes to Shireen's for a couple days every so often. But his father is *always home*. Oh, he rides his bike, gets groceries, once in a while even picks up the takeout. But they have not spent so much time in the house together since— since, well, never. Or maybe since he was one and (as it's been related to him, the subject somehow a little touchy) his father got a buyout and decided to hang with him for the summer before looking for a new job. But a baby, of course, is supposed to be in your way, a college student not so much.

"Jody wished me a good three-day weekend," his father says to him as he washes up the huge stack of dishes he just brought down from his room. It's the Friday before President's Day. His dad is reading the same magazine he's been looking at for, like, a week. "So I said oh my gosh, that's right, thank you for reminding me that I get to spend *a whole three days at home,* I've hardly been there for almost a year!"

He wants to say, you mean another three days with your too-old son practically up your butt? He wants to say, maybe if you actually ever went somewhere for real you wouldn't have to snark at Jody. He wants to propose an arrangement under which each of them promises to be out of the house, barring terrible weather, for the entire afternoon at least twice every week. Instead he tries to force a laugh, which won't come, so finally he says "I hear you". Which is lame but, well, his father has no more of a kick than he does.

"Want to take a walk?"

"I'm meeting Shireen at four. We're going to sit on a freezing bench ten feet away from Halie and talk to her for as long as we can all stand it."

His father glances at the clock. "That leaves time for a walk."

"You mean, like, around the block?"

"Sure, around the block."

How can he say no?

He is certain that his father has something in particular to tell him. But it turns out, incomprehensibly, that he just wants them to have nothing left to say to each other out on the sidewalk on a cold February afternoon as well as in every single room of the house over the course of almost a year.

Halfway around, as his father stops where he always stops to peer as he always peers down the narrow driveway between two triple-deckers to where the doghouse used to be, the one with the bulldog lying in it they would supposedly wave to when he was young, he says, "Dad? Can I ask a 'when you were my age' question?"

"Sure." Hard to tell with the mask (which is completely unnecessary alone outdoors with family), but his father seems surprised.

"Well, when you were my age, did it seem to you sometimes that maybe you shouldn't be where you were?"

A couple seconds of silence. "I don't follow."

"That even if you were supposed to be somewhere, it was somehow wrong."

More silence. "Got an example?"

Why did he start this? "Well, like this girl I know at school told me about a group she organized and I said it sounded interesting and she invited me to the next meeting. And when I got there it was obvious she never thought I'd show but she was glad to see

135

me, and the others were really welcoming and everything. But I spent the entire hour feeling like I was screwing it up for them by being there. Even though they thought they wanted me."

"What was it about?"

"That's not the point, Dad." They are rounding the last corner and in the home stretch. He very much wishes he had not sounded slightly annoyed, although truth, he sounds annoyed with his dad all the time and it never has any impact.

"Well, that's rough. I'm sorry."

"Was it like that for you, though?"

Quite a few steps in silence, there. Almost to the gate before his father stops dead, then: "You may not believe this, but it's hard to remember."

"You're kidding."

"No, I'm not." Their eyes meet above that mask. "I mean, maybe, sure, but … well, that time feels far, far away. I don't know if you realize this but I'm one of those people who've dealt with a lot of stuff by simply putting it aside."

"By 'putting aside' do you mean 'repressing'?"

"Not exactly. More like 'I have no reason to think about this ever again, so I won't'."

"Honestly, that doesn't sound like you at all, Dad."

His father laughs. "But it *is* me," he says, "whether you like it or not."

It took most of a year for their parents to meet. His folks—his mom especially—had been agitating to invite Amber for months, but he and Shireen felt shaky about it. Well, he did at any rate; he wondered at times if it was Shireen that shared his shakiness or (behind his back) her mom. Finally, in June, not long after school ended, his mother put her foot down—she said, "See? I'm putting my foot down" — and decreed that since it was so scandalously overdue he was to invite Amber *today* and no back talk. (It turned out surprisingly jolly; his father grilled sausages and those big mushrooms to go with his mom's famous potato salad and all five of them got a bit lubed up, none more so than his mother, who was usually one-and-done when it came to liquor, and Amber right behind her.)

"Well, I appreciate it in your mom," said Shireen as they walked to her house to deliver the invitation.

"Just basic courtesy, babe."

"Said the basis for all courtesy. I appreciate her persistence. We've been dodging it since Halloween, in case you forgot." She took his hand in the gentle way he enjoyed so much, like being touched by a cloud. "And it's not 'basic', putz, it's gracious. And sensible too, on account she knows her kid will never do better."

"Who could argue?"

She stepped suddenly in front of him and turned, taking both his hands in hers. "Baby doll, I think it's wildly unlikely that you comprehend even a hint of my gratitude and joy over you. Having you, knowing you. Touching you. *Looking at* you. I mean I make all these jokes and I am in fact pretty damn special but you really do not know what you've brought to my life."

He was a bit overwhelmed. OK, more than a bit. He'd been thinking they were about to reach a more serious stage and it was something he badly wanted. But finding her there already was a shock.

As he looked into her shining eyes and felt the warmth of her hands, wondering how he could possibly respond, she said, "Don't even try, beauty boy. Only leave it right there. So you don't forget what I said."

He has it. Son of a bitch. His father has it and is quarantining in their bedroom while he and his mother stay a million miles from each other although they both tested negative. She is sleeping in the basement; she insists. She is being very brave, in her descendant of pioneers way. He wants a hug from her so much, more than he has in years and years. Because every minute or two he remembers about his father. Fuck all.

"We can't be sure, honey," she says across their small living room, standing in the kitchen doorway while he watches her from the entry hall at the bottom of the stairs. He has just suggested that with masks and gloves it might be OK for them to briefly be near each other, touch each other. Since they're both negative. "The doctor said Tuesday, negative Tuesday means we're absolutely in the clear." She knows he knows this already, but has always believed in repetition.

"Dad said he's okay, right?"

She smiles, almost. "Call him yourself."

"No, please just tell me again."

"Sure. Yes, he feels fairly good. He does have a slight cough, he does feel tired, but no fever, oxygen's good. And he can still smell." It was her idea to find the very aromatic Yankee Candle Aunt Becca had brought last Christmas and leave it outside the door so her husband could put it by the bed and have an easy way to check. "Wouldn't I notice it when I ate?" his dad asked on speakerphone when she came back downstairs and called to advise. "That's only a few times a day," she said, "if that. You can sniff this every five minutes. Gives you something to do." He could see, even at a distance, the terrible effort she made to come up with a laugh, a real laugh, but she never quite got there.

Now he informs her: "Mine won't be negative."

"I'm sorry?"

He braces himself. "I said, my test won't be negative."

She shakes her head, studies him over her mask.

"What are you talking about?"

Wow. There is so, so much he could say. "I'm the one who brought it in here. I gave it to him."

She looks astonished, then concerned. "Honey, that's silly. We're hoping *he* didn't give it to one of *us*."

"No, Mom. Antibodies take longer in some people than in others. I know I'll be positive. I know it's my fault. Along with everything else."

"And I said that's silly. I've had more exposure than either of you! I understand how upset you are, dear, I am too, but this kind of thing is seriously not going to help." She starts to walk into the kitchen, then pauses and turns back.

"What do you mean," she carefully asks, "by 'along with everything else'?"

He gets out his phone. "I have an idea how it happened," he says. Maybe he is begging her to ask what the fuck's wrong with him, or trying to distract her. Maybe she's just a handy target. But he is certain he is breaking down at last. "I'm going to ask him about his movements. I'm sure I can prove it was me."

"You will not!" she says instantly. In the strange combination of whisper and shriek he's heard from her only a few times in his life. "He's worried enough as it is."

"He'll want to know."

"You will not call him!"

Things are getting out of hand—no, have *gotten* out of hand— and stupider by the moment, but he doesn't know what to do about it. He is upsetting her terribly. She deserves it less than anybody. Than *anybody*. He closes his eyes and with a supreme application of self-control manages to remain silent.

139

More calmly: "I am relying on you not to say anything of the sort to your father. And if you do you'll wish you hadn't."

This is truly freakish. A *threat*? From his *mom*? His eyes still closed, he pretends he is himself at six pretending to be a piece of furniture, doing everything he can not to move in the slightest. As he hears her turn and go into the kitchen, as he starts counting in his head, not even knowing how high he has to go to free himself from silent stasis, he begins to appreciate just how angry he is. He doesn't know which is the immovable object—himself or his anger—and which the irresistible force, but either way he's deep in trouble.

"Go fuck yourself, Mom," he whispers.

Something tells him, *open your eyes*. And he does. And she is not in the kitchen. She is standing there, mouth agape, looking at him.

They stare at each other—it's hard to know for how long on account of what he just said to his own mother, on account of every stress hormone he has ever had pouring into his body, on account of his having gone wild, scary wild—until he thinks he cannot bear it. If only she would come over and slap him silly. If only he could tell her how bad it's been. But now she is not staring, she is standing there weeping loudly, at least for her, which does the job far better than any slap.

He looks at his phone, then smashes it hard on the edge of the marble top of the antique hall table, twice. The second time he feels it crunch. It's done for, he thinks. He drops it on the floor, then takes his coat and scarf from the hook and goes out the door.

The street is plenty cold and it's starting to get dark. He spends considerable time walking aimlessly as it gets colder and darker, wishing he had his gloves and putting off the inevitable, namely telling Shireen what he did. When he finally gets there her bedroom window is dark but the kitchen is bright.

He hears the doorbell ring, hears the dog bark, hears Amber call "Coming!", pulls down his scarf so she'll know him in the dark.

"Hey!" she says as the light spills out, surprisingly cheerful. Maybe she's actually pleased to see him. He tries to smile back, but it can't be a success because her face changes instantly. "Reenie's not here, baby." It's her endearment for pretty much everyone, always, but this is the first time for him. The very first. "Didn't she tell you? She went to the mall with her cousin to get her other cousin—Lana, the pregnant one?—shower gifts."

"I lost my phone. Thought it might be here."

"I see," she says. "Well it's so *cold* out there! Come in."

The kitchen smells nice. She studies his face, now they're in the light. "They should be here soon. I made lasagna. Can you stay?"

"Um, thanks. I'm not sure. I should probably call my mom."

"Well you know where the old-type phone is," she says, turning and walking over to the range. She opens the door and peeks in. "Looking good! Hope you can join us."

"Amber?"

She turns back to him, still a little bent over. "Hm?"

"Do you like me?"

"What in the world?" She closes the oven and moves toward him until they are very far from safely distanced and certainly closer to each other than they have ever been. Much closer. "What kind of question is that?"

"An honest one," he whispers.

Her face fills with wounded love; her arms go all around him. "Oh my goodness, it's okay," she tells him, "it's okay. *It's okay.* My goodness, Joseph. You really need some crying don't you? Well I got you, so go ahead."

Learning to Dive

"Jumping is way better** than that inch by inch thing," says
Rosetta. "Just get it over with."

They all tread water following their coordinated leap, Emma to
her right and Rosetta to her left, for maybe half a minute before
Emma grabs one rail of a nearby ladder and Rosetta swims to the
other, leaving Grace with three options: keep her head above
water, fit herself between them, or drown.

"I like to dive in from up there," says Emma, pointing to the
deck at the deep end of the pool, a few yards away. "But it's too
crowded now. It's against the rules, but Janice said it's okay as
long as it's not crowded and I'm careful."

"She used to sit for you, right?"

"Yes she did, Rosie, and if I wasn't too old for it she still would,
but that doesn't mean she lets me do things other kids can't."

"I know, I was just curious."

"She would *never* do anything unfair like that."

"I said I *know*."

The sun seems brighter all the time; it's such a relief to be in the
pool in the surreal (well, climate change) heat of Memorial Day
2021, a real holiday at last instead of calling it one while
everybody hides at home. She can hear Janice doing a swim class,
a very young class at the "blowing bubbles" stage. She can even

make out the radio Aurea, the other lifeguard, is listening to at their table with the big red umbrella down at the shallow end.

"Curious why?"

"Oh *Emma*," says Rosetta with risky annoyance, "why do you *think*? Oh my god. She's totally snatched, she starred in like six high school shows when they still did them, she's going to *Princeton* in the fall. Nobody in their right mind would not want to be her and nobody normal wouldn't be curious."

"So why don't you ask me about her sex life?" says Emma, with the troublemaking grin they all know so well.

"What? What sex life?"

"What sex life? I dunno, Rosie, but I'm gonna say if she's sitting on our sofa with a guy when she thinks we're asleep a couple years ago and he's got his arm around her and they're making out and me and Boomer can see she's doing something with her hand and it's getting faster and faster that's called, um, *sex*."

"No!"

"Yes!"

"You let Boomer watch?"

Emma snorts in disgust. "Be real. If I'd so much as touched him he'd have screeched and then what?"

"Did the guy, um—"

"Well he sure was breathing heavy when she bent down—"

"Holy crap!"

"And in about half a minute there was a whole bunch of groaning and then she sat up again. So like I say I *think* that's what they mean by 'sex' and 'sex life'. Since you asked."

"Holy crap," Rosetta says again, but more quietly than before. Thoughtfully, in fact.

Hanging between them during that exchange was pretty funny. Not that she isn't as jazzed by Emma's play by play as Rosetta seems to be. "Was he good looking?" she asks.

"Well of course, speed bump. Janice can have her pick."

Rosetta winces but she doesn't mind a bit. She and Emma were practically in the womb together. She isn't even tempted to point out that a girl who is headed to Princeton might maybe pick for something other than looks.

"I never learned to dive," she says.

"You, Gracious? You're, like, a really *good* swimmer," says Rosetta, who seems very OK with the change of topic.

"Maybe. But I can't dive."

"I could ask Janice to teach you."

"That's a nice offer, Emma. I could probably even ask her myself. But I doubt she's going to teach me something against the rules."

"Oh, hell, I can teach you. It's the same as jumping except you get your feet right on the edge and jump forward instead of up."

"Thanks, Rosetta. Maybe the next time we're here when Emma thinks it's not too crowded the two of you can show me. If I watch you guys I can probably pick it up." She is well aware that she is "doing it again" as her big sister would say — that is, "sounding like a grownup throwing shade" — but her friends don't care and neither does she.

"Sure, Grace. Absolutely. You know, Rosie, it's true. This girl can pick up just about anything. *Like a used condom,*" she shouts, joined in unison by Rosetta. They are both instantly wild despite that was way back in early October, when they were only two days in-person, and should have been used up long since. But she's not bothered and it's nice to watch her friends laugh without masks, which she really missed all those months. As their giggles run down they look at her like she's flat dope and that's nice too.

"Emma!" calls Janice. They turn to see her shaking her head and the babies all staring at them. Janice scolding them for shouting the word "condom" after their recent discussion sets them off again, of course—Grace is chuckling herself—although they try desperately to stifle because having Janice say "Aurea, watch the students for a minute please" and come stalking toward them would be an *epic* disaster. They'd end up in the emergency room, declared dead on account of being dead.

Amazingly the condom thing made her sick (as sick as she would ever be, anyway) rather than hurt, like she kind of expected. She still feels like a child for not simply letting it lie there but instead picking it up in her gloved hand and walking it across the asphalt to the garbage can, not noticing how all alone in the middle she was until it was way too late; by the time she was halfway there they were all watching her and shortly after that shrieking with laughter. Ms. Weaver was chill enough to let the whole thing ride but made her private joke—"Well, Grace, I'd say you're a pretty good citizen to take *that* job on"— a little too loudly, which got them all going again. Later she wondered why Ms. Weaver, of all people, had used the word "citizen" and if that was part of what put everyone on repeat.

"Good times," says Emma, finally winding down. "Sorry, Gracette. You totally slay, no cap." Rosetta is nodding. She just smiles, though they hang there waiting. She can hear her father telling her *chénmò shì jīn*, silence is gold; she hears it maybe five times a day, but that is a big gain from when it was fifty and she practically never said anything at all. Esther can criticize what she "sounds like" all she wants, but life is a lot better now that she does *some* talking that people are always pretty much OK with and still knows the right times to keep quiet. In fact the only

reason Condom Day could have worked out so well instead of
setting her way back was that she said nothing whatever from the
moment the first kid laughed until she raised her hand in class,
half an hour after they came back inside, to answer a question
about leaf structure. And mostly kept her mouth shut at school for
a couple weeks after that so she wouldn't accidentally say the
wrong word, like "hat", and start the whole thing up again. And
never, ever replied to anything anybody said about it, nasty or
nice, except by smiling, either way. So score one for her dad, plus
Confucius or whoever was the first of the ten billion Chinese
people who said that in the last thousand years.

The worst thing, truly, about last spring—topping even the
lockdown and panic shortages and graphs getting scarier every
day and people practically throwing themselves across the street
when they saw each other coming—was not being with her
friends *at all* except in the stupid, lame, ridiculous zoom classes.
Or on the phone, which quickly seemed even more pointless than
ever. Class had minus zero in common with actual life; even kids
like her who were normally fine with being called on didn't want
to stand out on remote and the ones whose usual was barely
paying attention refused altogether on zoom, sometimes blatantly.
(Even some good students; she'd never been madder at Emma
than the time she caught her scrolling her phone—right there on
video!—while Ms. Monsky was talking about Ahmaud and
Brionna. What kind of crap was that for Little Miss Lefty, whose
granddad had been in something called SDS and was always
ranting about fascists and capitalist warmongers and white
supremacy?) But it was part of the special situation, she came to
understand; they all sat there like dolls, like crash test dummies,
protecting their secrets about whatever was happening at home
while Ms. Monsky went on and on, day after day, and it gradually

turned them into worse and worse versions of themselves. Sitting there hating their teachers for pretending this was school, hating the parents and siblings they were trapped with and couldn't rash on to their buds, hating each other for the distance and themselves for all that hate. Getting further and further apart. Because they were alone, really *alone*, and not zoom or instagram or tiktok or snapchat or *anything* could change that.

Rosetta looks at her, then Emma and asks "So what are we doing for lunch?"

"Angelo's?"

"Oh, Emma, haven't you had enough?"

"I suppose *you* want to hit Macca's, Rosie."

"Anything would be better than watching you try to eat cheese fries again."

This time Rosetta *has* gone too far. And will pay the price if not rescued. Dropping half an order of Angelo's bacon cheese fries, the rankest food known to humankind, into the lap of her favorite short skirt and all over her legs had definitely not enhanced Emma's cred. Fortunately Emma can take the hit but she sure doesn't want to be reminded.

"Well, *Rosetta*, if you—"

"I bet my mom would make us something," she says as loudly as she can manage.

They look at her. "You mean one of her Chinese things?" asks Emma.

"Well, yeah, I think so."

"Awesome!" says Rosetta.

At this moment being wedged between them deeply sucks, because she has no clue why she's hesitating and can't even look left or right without being literally in their faces. So she pretends she has something in her eye.

Truth, since Atlanta she's been surprised to find herself a little more nicked about words like "Chinese" and "Asian" (what does "Asian" even *mean*?) but it's never been a big thing in her particular life. Sure, now and then a white kid will be all weird or keep their distance but she's old enough to get that some white people are always handing out the shit and that others take a lot more and a lot worse than she does.

Anyway there's nothing wrong with Emma saying "Chinese things". That's exactly what the dishes are and her mother always calls them by their Chinese names, which of course Emma has no hope of learning. Her mother loves to cook for her daughters' friends, even if she and Es have their reasons for rarely asking her to, and they all love her and gobble her food when they can. She is as certain that Emma thinks Chinese is dank as she is that Ms. Weaver, who probably doesn't know her parents were never naturalized, is pro-immigrant and meant nothing by her "citizen" remark.

What really matters is that it's a nice, not a nasty, that Emma and Rosetta have so much fun shouting about the condom and that she actually believes they think she slays in some basic way. She also knows how much better it is to have an OG like Emma as fam than to actually be one; she is spared no end of bs from other kids but has no rep to keep up, except as GOAT of the wordless smile, which she feeds by making sure she does sometimes speak, but never in disapproval.

Esther often tries to bug her by calling her "sensitive" but it never works because she just isn't. The condom lift proves that, and other stories out of her life. She once overheard a girl say "Oh Grace doesn't get salty about *anything*" and that is exactly the way she wants it.

"Let's do it," she says, climbing the ladder at last. "She'll be way glad to see you."

The crappiest wasn't until October, though. Summer was a little better because they could get together outside. With the masks and everyone stupid jumpy and nothing to discuss except fear and complaint and not being able to do any of what they actually wanted it sure as fuck wasn't "normal", but at least she could see and hear them for real instead of on the damn phone and have actual proof they were OK and not about to drop dead.

For a while she wanted to suggest that they all ask their parents—her, Rosetta, Emma, Somayeh, Ebo, maybe Julie—could they please go together to one of the cheaper places in the gallery district downtown and sit in the new outdoor space at a slow time on a weekday, maybe calling ahead to request a big table set up as far apart as possible, if they promised to stop eating and put up their double masks the moment the server or anyone else came anyway near them and if the parents would give several rides each way so there were no more than two girls per car, with the windows open. But having thought it over for a couple of days she realized that the odds of her mother approving this were, like, way past forget it. And after another day she wondered what she'd been thinking; what a totally shit idea. Still, they could be together.

But then they started with "hybrid" and were pandemic-slapped all over again by the discovery that it was maybe a *little* better than all remote, the way getting your teeth cleaned was a little better than having cavities filled. And then it got too cold to sit shouting at each other from eight feet apart on benches at the park or playground equipment or the library steps. And when they realized there would be no trick-or-treating—not that they would have gone, they weren't babies anymore but they'd had

such wicked fun together for so many years, it was just uber-sad—
and that the holidays coming up would be way worse than that
because for parents the "festive season" was like Halloween on
PEDs and it would be awful for them to miss the usual family and
friends (never mind if there was someone who would be missing
forever), it was tough to find comfort in anything. Except when it
rained hard on a remote day so you could hope it would be nice
for in-person the next, which was pretty fucking pathetic, or when
another week went by without someone you knew getting it,
which while truly wonderful was actually no comfort at all.

"So Gracious," says Rosetta, as they wait for the walk signal at the
crossing by the little music store—Guitar Lessons Offered Here!—
that must be some kind of front or laundering op because it has
been there since like 1960 and looks it, and no one ever goes
inside, "is Jason around this weekend?"

She shakes her head almost invisibly. *Still* doesn't like the
name.

Emma laughs. "Don't be that way, *Rosacious*," she says, "you
know perfectly well he's not."

How do they know? She sure didn't tell them.

"He said they *might*, Emma."

"Nuh uh. He said they *would*. And they did, right Grace?"

"Sorry, Emma, who did what?"

Emma looks a little embarrassed, yes, but also sly. "Um, a
couple of weeks ago I was thinking maybe a function this
weekend, remember?"

"Yeah, kinda."

"Well all it was, was me and Rosie eyeballed Jasie at the mall
and I knew you'd want him there so—"

A horn honks nearby, startling them. The signal says WALK and an annoyed-looking woman with silver hair in a gigantic silver SUV really wants them to cross, judging by her urgent gestures. Emma goes instantly from embarrassed-but-sly to GO-FUCK-YOURSELF and turns her back on the driver.

"We'll cross when we fucking *want* to cross," she says, folding her arms. "What a tool."

Grace likes this Emma particularly. "That's straight," she says, reorienting in solidarity. Rosetta glances at the SUV and joins them.

Despite the heat the woman puts a window down to shout "I was trying to be *nice* to you little bitches!" and roars off.

She and Rosetta are totally dying but Emma runs a few yards after the SUV, shouting "*Whoa*! Nice flex, *Karen*!" She is already laughing harder than she has in many months when the victory bird Emma flips the woman as she turns into a side street, holding the pose for a couple seconds in case there's anyone else around to see, pushes her into a whole other zone, the one where you think you might pass out. It feels *good*. Rosetta is already on the sidewalk, passing out down there apparently, so she sits next to her, the two of them leaning on each other as they try to recover. Emma skips happily toward them.

Rosetta holds up her hand. "Please, Emma," she manages to gasp, "*don't say anything funny*." Emma sits facing them and smiles delightedly. "I was trying to be *boujee* to you little bitches," she says.

When it's over at last, when they have helped each other up and limped across the street and are walking towards the corner her house is four doors down from, Grace reboots. "So you asked him if you staged could he show and he said they were going to visit his mom's sister, right bff?"

"Right. They haven't seen her since last summer."

"And that's why no throwdown. Because you wouldn't have the power couple to headline. High key?"

Rosetta shakes her head to say she'd laugh if she weren't still flat out but Emma's eyes get big. "Damn Gina!" she says. "Gracette, you are finally developing some sass. Our little girl is growing up."

She'd been told his name was Jason but still could hardly believe it when Ms. Weaver wrote it on the board, his first day in class. It was *so* YA. As was the fact that he arrived two-plus months in, not only practically at Thanksgiving (a shit ton of boring books and movies had that setup) but smack in this big adult emergency when all the kids were still shook because if their teachers and parents were actually *fighting* over them—Ebo's mom, who used to teach high school, led them through the touchy questions all fall, including why almost every teacher over fifty was all-remote—who knew what could happen?

So it would have been chickenshit not to admit, once she hipped to herself, that the way she felt when she saw him was just as stale. Maybe more so.

It was important not to trip about it and especially to be totally 100—not to tell him or anyone else, no, that was the fast route to hell, but also not to put on or go extra or do anything any different than she would if she didn't care. This was trickier than it seemed because it's not so easy to hang chill, she found out, when the guy walks up while you are squadding. The Smile is one thing as her ticket to keeping her mouth shut and another as cover. She had a really close call when he stopped by their table at lunch and as he was walking away—he might still have been near enough to hear, even—Emma said "Goals, huh Grace?" and Ebo snorted soda all over herself. Knowing she had to do *something* she asked "So what do you like most about him, Emma?", a pretty good shot that made the whole table go weak as Emma insisted "Yo, you *know* I'm tight with Tommy" and eyed her. As if it hadn't been Luke before Tommy and Mario before that. When they quieted down she said "Sorry, just me being all fomo" which of course made Rosetta say "Don't stress, Gracious, your turn's any time" so mission accomplished. Later on, hanging on the library steps with Emma she was *very* tempted to spill. But she got a grip when she thought about how Emma—who probably, no definitely knew it was the shit in the first place and decided to cut her a break— could keep something low for about a day and a half max and told herself, as she so often did, that if you zip you always have the option of spilling, but once you spill there is no getting it back.

As they come up to the house she sees at the top of the driveway the lawnmower no one will touch, not even Sally who now cuts their grass every two weeks, and snarls inside. Almost a year! Impossible, she thinks for the trillionth time as she leads them up the walkway and around the house to the kitchen door. It's more like ten thousand. Or maybe one day. She is very much *not* looking forward in any way to *jì chén*, to being dragged backwards into something she can't defend herself against, and though they haven't discussed it she knows her sister feels the same. Even her mother would probably agree, if she were honest, but Grace understands that for her parents and people like them that stands for nothing compared to ritual. Her mother talked a bunch about heaven and all that a year ago (although she believes none of it) and will soon, she knows, start talking about it again, and they will have to take food and whisky and leave it there for the staff to clear away within hours, she is sure, and burn money which must be *majorly* against the rules. The whole thing will be humiliating as well as unbearable. A twofer.

God damn. It was almost too hot to hold.

"Jesus, Gracie," said Jason, in a tone that confused her. Wasn't this what guys wanted?

It was April and blessedly no longer 2020 and the back yard was warm, at least warm enough to sit there with someone other than family for the first time since the horrible shit began and it was dark because her mom was still thrown off by the time change so had not yet hit item seven on her nightly Paranoia Checklist by turning on the too-bright, too-sensitive motion detector light, the one her dad had repeatedly promised to install a timer on but never had, and hearing through a window that was somehow still open her sister and mother washing up in the kitchen meant they would not be interrupted. The first time had been so awkward, *brutally* awkward—really it was no wonder, she had last spring to get past plus a couple weeks this March sneaking around with him at her own whack insistence, holding hands when no one could see because why? something wrong with her having a boyfriend? and then going pub and everyone *smiling* at them all the time like *oh*, how *sweet*—and it was kind of a miracle they were trying again but tonight the warmth in his voice and the soft kissing and his arm around her shoulders and gentle hand on her breasts were so nice, *so nice*. It was definitely what *she* wanted right now, even if he didn't; she was totally into it and wasn't about to stop.

"*Fuck*, Gracie," he whispered. His hand got less gentle but she liked that too.

"Want me to stop?"

"Shit no."

"Thank you for making us lunch today, Mama," she says, in the careful way she's heard herself talking to her mother for quite a while. Her mother looks a little sharply at her, which also happens a lot. As if she suspects, but barely, a problem she doesn't know how to approach.

"You can bring them any time, *qiān jīn*, you know that. I wish you would bring them more."

"Mama, at my age in America you don't usually bring your friends home all the time."

"At my age in America! Do you know how often you say that to me now?" Her mother is cooking dinner. She is *talking to the stove*, her father's phrase of years ago that stuck with her and Esther. "What age is that, girl? And where is this 'America' you keep telling me about? And how did you learn so much about what every single child there does and does not do? Set the table." When she was younger she would say *Don't talk to the stove, Mama* but now it's easier to just let her.

"I say that because I'm older, I'm not a baby anymore," she says as she gathers the placemats and plates. "And being older here means different things than it meant for you in China thirty years ago."

"I know very well you are not a baby," says her mother, suddenly turning her head and smiling, brightly but briefly, before attending to her pan again. "Like you should know I am not an idiot. I understand it's different and that I don't know much about it. Which is one reason I want you to bring Emma and the others."

"We don't say in front of parents what we say when we're by ourselves."

Her mother stamps her foot. "You *do* think I'm an idiot! Go set the table, Grace."

She does as she's told, lost in thought about Janice and the guy on the couch and her near certainty that Emma's gossip, for all she tried to make it about Miss Princeton, was a tell that she is getting down heavy herself now. She's certainly been holding Tommy's string long enough. Maybe Rosetta (who mostly moves carefully) was thinking not of her own future but Emma's present. About her Gracious she can't possibly be wondering. Can she?

When she returns to the kitchen for the chopsticks and water glasses her mother is standing there watching her come in, holding the pan, on the verge of tears or rage which have never been that different for her anyway.

"How can you not understand me? Are you too stupid to know I was a girl myself? Can you tell me the wrong in a mother in my position doing her best to be close to her daughters? Your sister is the same. I would be ashamed to have anyone hear what you say to me."

No, she is the one who is ashamed, who hangs her head, whose gut suddenly hurts, a lot, who feels like she's dropped nine or ten years in a moment and is a child being scolded for putting something in the toilet. She stares at the floor. No, she would not want anyone to hear it either.

"I'm so sorry, Mama. You're right. I am so sorry to be disrespectful." When she looks up her mother's tears have started but are already stopping. Gathering her every bit of courage she approaches and opens her arms, closes her eyes. *Oh please. Please.* She stands there like a cormorant with its wings out to dry on a rock in the pond by the cabin they used to rent from her dad's work friend. She has no real idea how long it is before the pan hits the burner and she feels the precious relief of her mother's arms going around her, but it seems a long time. Or how long they stand that way, except it's even longer.

159

"When was it?"

A warmish early March afternoon and they were finally alone, after several months of her hiding and Jason seeking more or less every day, the poor guy. They were sitting together on a low wall, his suggestion as he was walking her home after she'd finally agreed to it (though she had no intention of letting him get anywhere near the house). The situation was far from a surprise, she'd been imagining it forever, but she was panicking anyway and really it didn't help for him to ask that. She'd have thought he was playing except for the respectful way he said it.

"What? I mean, what it?" She was squirrelly as fuck. She had never sounded like such a fool.

"My old man," he said, sighing and pausing, looking up at the sky, "went down before we hardly knew what a coronavirus was."

"Oh," she said. "Was he sick for a while?"

He shook his head. "Not really. Less than a week. Four days with my sister and me in one part of the house and my mom and dad in the other, one day in the hospital thinking now everything will be okay, one day of this nurse trying to get my sister on facetime so we could say goodbye."

She was already crying.

"I guess it was a lot easier than him getting cancer and suffering for months and all that," he said. Then shook his head. "No, it wasn't. It was like being kicked in the face. Kicked hard."

He looked at her like he was still waiting for her to answer and all she could do was sit and cry. She didn't know who'd told him. She didn't know if she was crying for his father or her own or for all the days she'd spent pretending whatever, she couldn't even *remember*, just so she could get through them. She wasn't sure whether sitting so close to someone who'd been dealing with the same thing all the while was intolerable or some kind of opening or maybe both. She wanted to speak but knew for sure that if she tried she would sob so loud the whole town would hear. Which would be OK with the town, probably, but not with her.

To her major shock he sighed again and took her hand. He was crying too. They sat crying together, holding hands and she thought, *this is beyond.* Whether it was that or his warm hand and endless (it seemed) patience or the minutes steadily passing she was finally able to speak. They were both still crying, but not in the helpless way.

"It was totally like that, Jason," she said. "I mean it was June and it was different, he went to the hospital right away and was there almost two weeks and about ten days in they said he would get better and then he didn't. But the facetime thing. And what you said about the kick?"

"Ever make you want to hurt someone?"

Shaking her head, she was surprised not by the question but by her willingness to answer. "I just wanted to forget him."

"But it doesn't work like that."

"No," she said, hopefully, her head resting lightly on his shoulder, "it doesn't."

Fast

He's waiting on red wondering how to kill another hot, boring Saturday when she blows past him on a Trek. Just as the light changes. He floors it, then slows to match—she's only doing twenty-four!—as he comes abreast.

"She's fast, she's shapely, she's blond," he announces, accelerating away. "The rest doesn't matter."

Top of the street is still green. He spots an open space to stall in just before the corner but when he gets there it's a hydrant, as he very fucking well knows and has for years. So he can *pretend* to be parking there then "change his mind" and pull out behind her. He feels pretty clever as she coasts between him and the Honda at the curb, shooting him a wave for leaving her room, then not so much when she quickly passes in front of him and turns left a hair before red. Damn.

But he'll get his shot anyway, it turns out. Because she pulls over on the far side and heads for the rack next to the mailbox, in front of the bank. Like she's *going in to use the ATM*. Fuck yes. They can give him twenty fifty-dollar tickets for parking by the hydrant, he'll come back and move it soon but first things first.

Ignoring (but not easily) the apparent disapproval of a gray-haired woman in a lime green sundress, he rushes across the street as the walk light is counting down 4, 3, 2 ... to find her still in the lobby, plenty of time. And when he joins her it's better than that. Because it looks like the ATM is *down*. And she's annoyed.

"You're kidding," he says.

"Not our lucky day."

"Let me try."

"Forget it," she says, putting out her hand to keep him from sliding his card in, which he is pretending to be about to do. "You'll only lose it."

"Thanks," he tells her. "I guess it's *my* lucky day, anyway, having you here to stop me."

She isn't especially cute but her smile pretty much makes that irrelevant. Plus he likes the sound of her voice. And she isn't all stiffened up from being closed in a small stuffy space with a strange guy.

"Another bank around here?"

Well, the whole place is banks.

"Sure, there's one up the block. And it's got A/C, I think." He hopes she won't take this as a comment on her sweatiness. The truth is he loves sweat on the right person. Such as this one. He holds the door and gestures her through, which in his experience makes a good impression on almost everyone.

"Hey," he says as they head up the street, wishing it was the south side because it's well over eighty and the sun is already murder, "it was you I passed on your wheels just now, right? Going fast as hell?"

"It wasn't that fast."

"I ride myself, and it was definitely fast."

"I can go faster."

"About to ride not that fast somewhere else?"

"Why do you ask?"

He points at her helmet.

"Oh!" she says, stopping and unbuckling it. "What a tool! I'm always forgetting and people laugh. I guess it's my lucky day too, that you're here to remind me."

She's fast, she's shapely, she's blond, she smiles like a state fair in full swing and *she calls herself a tool*. What a find!

"I do it too. But I was wondering if this is maybe a stop on a longer ride."

"Well I did come from across the river. But on an errand here. And just now remembered I'm supposed to have cash."

"Doesn't it frost you when they say 'cash only!' and give you the *hey stupid* look?"

"I just never go back there."

"Excellent policy."

They've reached the next lobby. In which a guy their age whose hair is practically long enough to jump rope with—how can he stand it in this weather?—is using one of the two machines. He'll have to make his move soon.

She stops outside the door and pulls a mask out of her pocket. Catching his look, she shrugs and says, "Delta. You know."

"As it happens I just had a negative test. But I could have been infected."

"Wow. You're so right. I should have put it on before."

Here we go. "But then I wouldn't have seen the most brilliant smile ever. So I'm seriously glad you didn't."

OK, she blushes a little. He puts his own mask on and she slips her card into the reader.

"I'm Will," as the lock buzzes.

"Kate," as she pulls open the door and gestures him through.

A few of his associates managed to somehow get the impression that as far as he was concerned the relationship was already over, that delaying the first shot was his way of provoking a split. Although he chose not to correct them, this was not only untrue (at least at an intentional level) but would have been cowardly and small. While he couldn't entirely explain why he didn't simply click the link when it arrived, he knew the endless stream of "When we're both fully vaccinated" comments (up to and including "we can find a place together" and "you can finally meet my folks") he'd been enduring for months was only one of multiple factors. "It's complicated," he would have said if anyone had been listening.

Vaccination aside, though, it made things tough. If she'd surfaced it with something like "It'll be weird to start thinking about all the normal relationship stuff again, won't it?", which was the approach he'd been planning, he'd have had less of a problem. But she'd shown clearly that she just didn't appreciate their situation, namely that there might not have been any relationship without the virus. They were only part-way in (he'd been all the way in only twice) when the shit hit the fan; yes they were both hot for it and certainly would have hooked up a few more times regardless but having already been mutually exposed it was natural to look to each other for all sorts of companionship along with sex during the early, panicky, isolated stage. Timing is everything, right?

And it quickly became a habit. Ginnie was fun. She lived four blocks away and even that short walk soon seemed a pointless formality when she was the only one he had to ride and eat and netflix with; by early May they were spending as much as a week or so at her place, then at his, with a day or two off in between. So the usual "screwing aside, do I like them enough to stick with it?" hadn't even been asked. By either of them. Which bothered him mostly on her account, honestly; getting along with him seemed way easier for her than it maybe should have been.

Not that he didn't like her a lot. She was kind, passionate about the right causes, funny as hell, and a damn good conversationalist. Not to mention a looker who really wanted to fuck, most days anyway. If he'd been asked to review her last April it would've been five stars all the way. But no matter how you match up you still have to make a deliberate decision. Which they hadn't. Other than that they'd rather not be alone.

So in truth what made him resort to stonewalling the vax to the point at which they were having long, stupid arguments about it was that the relationship didn't actually exist, at least not as she understood it, that everything she said was based on a fantasy too big and false for him to address with the tact and sensitivity he would require of himself. Like how he wasn't going to tell Aunt Ruthie that the "rigged election" was a malicious self-serving lie. It called for an emotional face slap he was in no way willing to deliver. Therefore yeah, OK, maybe it *was* a cowardly provocation on his part. But definitely not small, in fact almost larger than life.

"So what's the errand?"

He likes her partial eye roll. "I could tell you anything," she says. "But the truth is I've busted my screen *three times* this year. And the only place that was open and I could get at until recently is crazy expensive. So I came over here to go to what's-it-called —"

"Phone Aid."

" — right, because they're silly cheap. But cash only. Which means I just took out pretty much my last dollar."

Here we go, take two. "Which means I'll have the pleasure of buying you lunch." As she starts to speak he holds up a minimal hand. "I'm totally down with you treating next time. But if you think I'm missing the chance to hang with a wicked fast rider who seems like a lot of fun because she happens to be randomly broke at the moment, well … okay, you don't know me. But I'm not."

Her laugh—after a beat of silently looking at him—is simply delightful. And would be even if he weren't feeling so delighted with himself.

"Okay, thank you."

"You vegan?"

"No, but I'm not especially into meat."

"Me neither. You know Veggie Heaven?"

"Heard about it."

"So here's my proposal." He winces internally at his word choice, then sees she is hiding her amusement. How charming is that? "We're almost to Phone Aid. And as it happens I have a book waiting for me at the library, around the corner. There's almost always a line of serial phone abusers" (making her giggle is *so* cool) "and I'm betting I'll be back before you're through. But whoever gets done first will wait in front of the phone shop. Okay?"

She nods solemnly, then looks impressed. "You're giving me a chance to bail."

"Well, yeah. I put you on the spot."

"And I agreed."

"Why should I draw my own conclusions when I can leave it up to you?"

Speaking of injections, she doles out this magnificent beaming of hers like a smack dealer giving out samples and he is already addicted. They have just arrived at Phone Aid when she hits him with it again and says, "You seem like a truly nice guy, Will. A sweet guy. See you in a few." Then disappears inside, while he grins like a total idiot. This is becoming slightly scary.

He always considered himself rebellious. Or felt he wanted to be. Or hoped people would think he was. Whatever, it created a lot of difficult situations, from an early age. For somewhat obscure, maybe even incoherent reasons being compliant usually felt disingenuous, even shameful, and refusing to go along like a win.

He'd gotten mostly on top of this since he left home for college, but the lockdown presented a tailor-made temptation to backslide that grew more compelling as the calamity developed. When people crossed the street to avoid him he shook his head and had to stop himself from calling out, "It's six feet, not twenty-five." He wanted to refuse the hand sanitizer at Trader Joe's (which he could have done, but at the risk of an unpleasant scene) and *did* refuse to follow the one-way signs in the aisles. He biked maskless by the river for the first couple of months until it became very clear that this was truly a shithead move that a lot of people hated, plus Ginnie stopped coming along because of it.

So he put on the fucking mask. And for similar reasons had given in on most of the rest by July. And over the ensuing year, if he was honest, what was left never really added up to rebellion, more like being a petty jerk. Because sure, he was prone to pushing back but he also was a smart, educated person who definitely believed in science and considered himself rational about risk. So he settled on safety-valving the subversive tendency with a few small, regularly repeated "acts of conscience" that no one even noticed—such as walking into a seat-yourself lunch place without a mask and going right to a table, or looking annoyed when a server started in with the ritual sanitation—and found himself able to live more or less comfortably with doing the right thing.

On the other hand ... among his friends and especially Ginnie's, practically the entire fucking city in fact, the only thing that would have been more outrageous than refusing the needle would have been joining Aunt Ruthie's boyfriend (what a waste of boomer space!) at the Capitol insurrection. And having lots of time to consider this while he waited for older and less healthy folks to get theirs, plus feeling a pressing need to compensate for having stood staunchly with the majority — that is, to relieve the pressure in a larger way, so he wouldn't eventually blow — he at some point nailed it down.

And thus by late July, by the Day of the Brilliant Smile (as he thought of it forever after), the date he'd finally selected for getting the first shot was still three weeks away and he was still having himself tested every three or four days, as he had since late May in anticipation of the people he used to hang with pre-COVID (and pre-Ginnie) expressing their newly vaxed status and where the fuck is the party? With a good many consequences, predictable and otherwise, some of them still rolling in.

When he comes around the corner she is standing there, shoulders against the wall and hands behind her back, looking insanely fucking winsome. As he reaches her she steps out and matches his stride and they walk towards Veggie Heaven together.

"I'll be honest," he says on impulse. He absolutely can't hide the effect she's having and needs to state some smaller version or he'll spill the whole thing and freak her out. "A woman riding really fast excites me."

"I'll be honest too — I kinda assumed that's why you paced me to check me out."

Holy shit. "You're kidding! You knew the whole time that I followed you into the bank?"

"Yeah."

"And that didn't bother you, Kate?"

He sees the use of her name register. "Look, it's been a long fucking pandemic. I don't know you well enough to go through the gory details but even for a modern girl there are times when it's nice to be wanted. And this turned out to be one of them."

"Turned out to be?"

She laughs, and it washes him like the intense sunlight as they cross. "That was *so* cute when you pretended to be shoving your card into a dead ATM!" Now it's him blushing. "And then you talked up my riding, which since I happen to know I *am* pretty fast I took as sincere."

This is more than simple luck, he is realizing. Like, maybe life-changing.

A man is shepherding two helmeted children on scooters towards them and obviously feels the sidewalk is way too crowded to be safe, so he very briefly touches her shoulder to guide her aside until they pass. And when they have says, "Wait a minute," and stops and turns. "You deliberately left your helmet on!"

"What you said was endearing and I wanted to do the same."

"Because reciprocity?"

"Just because."

"But please tell me," he says, realizing he has not sounded so sincere in a long, long time, "that calling yourself a tool is something you normally do."

"It is." She is happily grinning. "And I could tell you really liked it."

OK, fuck it, that's all he can stand. He reaches out to take her hand and she meets him halfway. The sidewalk actually is pretty crowded and being in contact definitely makes it easier to navigate.

"How far to Veggie Heaven?" she asks.

"Half a block."

"So we'll do this until we get there."

173

"Agreed."

"Actually," she says, after thirty of the best seconds he's had in years, "let's go move your car away from that hydrant first." She giggles. "Oh for god's sake, don't look so ashamed! It doesn't make you Saddam Hussein. Or even a tool. And from my point of view it was flattering as hell."

"It's two blocks farther up."

"That much more time to hold my hand."

He was very grateful that it happened—broke into the open for good—in the park on a gorgeous June day with lots of people around, which kept it under control. He suggested they sit on a bench but she wanted to be farther from him than that, it seemed, so they had the conversation (if it could be called that) under the big aspen not far from her building, more distanced than he'd deliberately been from anyone he was actually talking to since the whole thing started.

"You know what? This is the end."

"If you're saying so, I guess it is."

Her weeping honestly seemed way overdue. "Don't try to make it my fault."

"I swear I'm not. Go ahead and call me names. Like *asshole*. Or how about *stinking bastard*? I won't argue."

She stared at him in wonder as she wept, and for just a moment he felt not only regret but doubt.

"Although I still can't believe you've made such an enormous unclimbable mountain out of one temporary molehill."

"You're the one who did that."

There was no argument on earth to counter a statement so accurate, so he wasn't going to try. He knew he should walk away but couldn't bring himself to it yet.

174

"I do love you, Ginnie."

"Oh!"

Her expression of pain was very clear and very painful. "Yeah. You're right. I'm sorry."

As he watched her make a massive effort to reassert self-control he realized he'd seen her do this in a small way many times. Apparently this was the big one she'd been practicing for.

"We're at a parting of the ways, Will. That you couldn't change even if you wanted to, which you don't. So saying *love* is not only a *stinking bastard* thing to do, an *asshole* thing to do, it's not at all to the point. Which is that the contempt you've shown me is too hard a face slap to ignore. So fuck you and your love."

She turned quickly and walked a couple of steps, then spun around long enough to say "I *used to* love you" before turning again and rounding the bend, out of sight.

Eventually he is very hungry, hungry as sin, not having eaten breakfast or lunch because they never get to Veggie Heaven. After reaching his car—where she runs to grab the ticket off the windshield and skips out of reach, waving it in the air and saying "My treat!" while a bunch of people waiting outside the Brook-Lynn Diner watch them from across the street, then knocks him silly by holding it out and when he takes it refusing to let go and staring into his eyes for a long moment before walking around to the passenger door where she waits to be let in—and parking it a couple blocks away, they look at each other and just keep walking in the same direction, all the way to the river and back, taking a break from quietly holding hands only long enough to put each other's numbers and instagrams in their phones. More than once he considers confessing his great delay, his perverse recalcitrance, but there'll be time for that later. Which is also what he tells himself when he is reminded by the fancy McDonald's sign that they are not far from their starting point and is swept by a powerful wave of regret that he didn't suggest going to his place when they got into the car.

"And now I'll be very majorly honest," she says as they stand by her Trek Domane, watching each other carefully. "Much as I'd like not to."

Fucking shit! She's got someone already! But it's even worse.

"I'm about to move to Ohio," she tells him, looking other than cheerful for the very first time. "My sister died there last year."

"Your sister?"

"My big sister Sally," she says with what might be the saddest, weakest smile in her range. "I know, right? Big Sally and her l'il sister Kate, sounds like a bad country song. But that's how it was. I haven't even gotten started on really missing her yet."

"Oh my god, Kate. How awful. My god. I'm so sorry." He is not sure which part is more awful. Each by itself feels like more than he can bear.

"Her husband can't handle the kids on his own. He's been trying so hard but he can't. And he has no one. No one but me."

He'd like to believe he is happier for the brother-in-law and his children than he is devastated for himself. But it's a major reach at best.

"I'm glad he has you."

"Yeah. Me too."

They stand in silence for some time, for once not looking at each other.

"So this is a parting of the ways, I'm afraid," she says at last.

"Parting? They haven't joined yet."

"No?" She looks down at their hands, holding each other. Which for some reason makes him let go.

"I'm pretty sure I'll be back. Before *too* long. Honestly, I hope I will."

"Can I see you before you go?"

"I'm sorry, I don't know how. I'm leaving early Tuesday and there's a shit ton to do." He wants to beg her for half an hour, somewhere in there—a tiny percent of the total!—but crushed and desperate as he is he knows that would be just too pathetic, even for someone as understanding as he believes her to be.

"Look, Will," she says. "I don't know what's going to happen. I just don't. Yeah, we could probably find half an hour. And I'd say let's exchange email or something. But frankly this has been so nice—I mean really, unexpectedly lovely—that I don't care to mess it up by forcing it. We hardly know each other but we've both made an awesome impression. Can we leave it that way? For now?"

"For now might be for always."

"It might," she concedes. "I hope it won't." She takes his hand again, making him sorry he ever let go. "When I say 'lovely' I mean *lovely*, Will. Thank you."

Then he stands there like a powerless fool as she holds his hand, releases it way too soon, puts on and buckles her helmet, kisses his cheek, unlocks her bike and wheels it to the curb and mounts. With one foot on the pedal she looks back at him, somehow conjuring a smile that puts all the others to shame, that covers the whole scene in glory, and says "Timing is everything, right?" Then she is off, going fast enough to take his breath away.

Reunion

"**S**o Zbiszek," says **Tami**, carefully lifting a loaded potato skin from their impressive-looking appetizer platter of skins, wings, and what the menu calls bruschetta but Jim would characterize more as homemade French bread pizza without the sauce but with a great deal of mozzarella, "when do you fly?" To everyone in the US other than fellow Poles the man is known as Bish, which he adopted early on because a name beginning with Zb is just too awkward for most Americans, but Tamila of course calls him Zbiszek. Sometimes even Zbigniew, which Zbiszek is the diminutive of, something she made a point of becoming informed about the first time they met. Just as she refuses to indulge white people's discomfort over unfamiliar names by allowing them to imagine hers is "Tammy"; only Jim can call her Tami, and god help him should he ever introduce her that way.

Zbigniew Pawel Wyszynski is needless to say every bit as white as James Norcross Jenkins but very not American, which is what counts, at least to Tamila Abigay Walker and Bish; the immigrants mutually enjoy contrasting their "just visiting" (for over thirty years) status with the unpullably deep roots of Jim and Julianna Rainsford Stratton, who are both as WASP as it gets, although he can't definitively trace his ancestry back to the Massachusetts Bay Colony before 1675 whereas she can do it on

181

both her mother's and her father's sides. "It was random,"
Julianna once explained. "They met at the roller rink at seventeen
and were going steady before they got around to discussing their
Puritan forebears. But when I tell people they think it's a
conspiracy."

"Friday evening," says Bish, having stripped off the last of his
wing and left the bones on his bread plate. "Assuming the
Lufthansa ground handlers don't strike. And you?" He is going to
Poland to visit his son, whom he has not been anywhere near in a
year and a half and who refuses to come to the U.S. although (or
maybe because) he is a native-born American who never set foot
in his father's land of origin until he was twenty-four. "He likes
Krakow," Bish replied, shrugging, to Jim's inquiring look when he
first explained his plans. "I'm just glad he's happy and wants to
see me." For her part, Tamila is terribly excited to be returning to
Jamaica and her parents for the first time in over two years but is
unlikely to admit that to anyone but Jim for fear of activating all
sorts of American stereotypes of Caribbean peoples of color;
before she knows it they'll have her dancing on a rooftop, singing
in a parodic Jamaican accent about where she likes to be.

"Also Friday evening!" she tells Bish. "What time is your
flight?"

"Half-past nine."

"Oh, I'll be long gone by then," she says with regret, as if
partying it up at the international terminal is a favorite recreation.
"Mine's around seven."

"Seven-twenty," says Jim.

"Thank you dear one. I believe that falls within the bounds of
'around seven', but it's good to know you have it loaded in
memory." Although this is definitely sarcastic it is also very
affectionate and Tami takes his right hand, which is lying on the

table, in her left. "I'm going to miss him terribly," she tells Bish and Julianna. "I always miss him terribly."

"It seems obvious you would," says Julianna.

He squeezes her hand; he'd like to kiss her but that's still too demonstrative for him, at least at dinner. She is always showing people how she treasures him and it moves him every time. Beyond the pride involved he fiercely appreciates her frankness, in fact idealizes her for it. Over the years, he's come to recognize, she has continually inspired him to at least try not to be the man his upbringing marked him for, the careful man of few words sitting and watching others live. To this day he has no clue what could possibly have interested her in him and fully accepts that he will never have her energy, her presence, her expressiveness or courage. But he has surely become more open, which gives him at least a fair shot at being more like her generally. And in recent years, settling into what he now understands to be the age of relative wisdom, he is focusing this more intently; having acknowledged with distaste how often he still hid, fibbed, and passively misled to avoid both minor trouble and the consequences of displaying true emotion, he is on a campaign to change his ways. What would Tamila do? She'd be herself—that is, honest. So *be honest* is his slogan (it's shorter and more honest than *be authentic*, which he also considered) and though he still sometimes feels ridiculous telling himself this, it's astonishing how greatly it increases the odds of his looking back on each day with satisfaction rather than regret.

The server arrives bearing their plates. "Praise the lord!" says Bish, throwing up his hands in mock elation, and they all laugh. When Jim compares their steaks to his chicken parmigiana, though, he feels like a fool. The careful man still manages to deprive him of fun from time to time; it's a never-ending struggle.

As they all dig in he is again amused by what an odd lot they are. He never imagined that the very first couple they hosted at their house after they were both fully vaccinated would be Julianna and Bish, but that was the way it worked out, at the end of May, with the four of them getting not inconsiderably drunk over roast pork and tiramisu. And now they're having dinner again just two months later at a popular neighborhood steakhouse very close to Julianna and Bish's home that Jim and Tami happen to like a lot but rarely visit. Julianna made the reservation and invited them, so here they are.

They are not really close friends, although he wants to treat Julianna as a closer friend than she is for several reasons, most perfectly sound but one a bit shameful in a mundane, everybody does it sort of way. She makes him laugh, she has interesting takes on larger events and her daily experiences which she expresses briefly but well, sometimes with fresh insight, and as far as he can tell his attention genuinely gratifies her; apparently she too wants to be closer, although they never seem to make progress. He believes they are similar in many respects and likes to think they tacitly understand each other. He also wants to be closer because she is beautiful—just short of strikingly, but in a way that having gained your attention refuses to release it—and has the incontrovertible poise of someone who has always been so and has always known it. On top of this there is invariably an extraordinarily fresh aspect to her appearance that despite her reasonably age-appropriate graying hair and wrinkles puts her in a class by herself. Even her coats and shoes always look brand-new. As Tami once put it, "There are plenty of great-looking people in their fifties—"

"For instance *you*, dear."

"Thank you darling—but we all have wear and tear on us. Except Julianna hasn't."

While he isn't proud of the looks thing—and even less so of the fact that, as he has forced himself to concede, her unmarred aspect represents for him the most discreditable sort of personal challenge—he's glad he can at least *be honest* with himself about it, and is absolutely sure it isn't looks alone. If he's honest at a different and more important level, he quite likes her. He would like her more if she laughed once in a while (although she does smile affectingly), if he didn't feel she was at all times at least slightly cautious, if she were not inexplicably reluctant to talk at length about her work (she is a law school professor and he chief counsel to a large, well-known NGO), but he likes her easily enough to enjoy a little banter, as in their texts earlier that day:

> Are we still on for tonight? 6.30 at Mike's?

wouldn't miss it for the world, Julie. does anyone ever call you that?

Julianna seems so formal. Julie emphasizes your sparkling side

> Hooray!

> Jules is what my best friends call me, so call me Jules 🖤

> not sure if Jules shows my sparkling side, but what a nice thing to say!

it does. and I am dedicated to drawing out your sparkling side, Jules

> [longish pause]

185

> Are you flirting with me, Jim?

yes, but harmlessly

Clearly her last message went beyond banter, and of course threw him a bit. He has indeed been flirting with her here and there for years but she's never before shown any sign of noticing. Still he feels he answered her adroitly, no one else will ever see it, and most important it represents only a small but interesting change in their dynamic that will go no further, Julianna being Julianna, as long as he doesn't push it, which being Jim he certainly won't.

On waking the following morning it comes to him that she has left him the last word before, and he is surprised by his markedly mixed feelings; while he already regrets their having crossed even a faint, preliminary line, he has no desire to cross back. So when his phone buzzes he grabs it off the night table with a sort of eager foreboding. But it isn't Julianna, it's Tami from the kitchen:

> a brilliant evening! thanks so
> much Julianna

to which Julianna replies:

> So wonderful to see you!

and Jim finds he can't resist:

regretting not getting steak
so we'll have to do it again
soon :)

which to his bemusement draws a message just to him:

> Any time!

looking forward to it, Julie

(i decided that "best friends"
name privileges are great
but "idiosyncratic personal"
name privileges are even
better)

> Yes, I was thinking the same.
> Julie is a-ok by me.
>
> I'll still call you Jim to your face,
> but for us you've been Jimmy
> Jenks since we heard your
> nephew call you that.

wouldn't mind your calling
me Jimmy. and I'm quitting
Julianna, you are much more
a lively Jules/Julie sort of
person

And again radio silence. What is she thinking? That she can take it back? There's no way he can forget it whether she wants him to or not.

Tamila, with her reliably keen intuition for what's on his mind, spends the next three days teasing him about keeping his distance from Julianna while she and Bish are away. "No steak for two!" she says with a grin. Talk about lively! Joyous Tamila—with her arresting deep eyes and strong legs and laugh like a waterfall, his only hope of not becoming a quieter, fainter version of himself in old age as his parents did—is teasing him about timid Julianna, every bit as whitebread bland as Jim himself and even more chronically unexuberant.

And she does it out of a sort of blissful ignorance. The woman really has no idea that a persistently adolescent part of him still asks every day how she can possibly be his. Tami was out of his league to begin with and he is aging far less gracefully so the gap keeps getting wider. The years are touching her, certainly, but not to her detriment; she is still magnificent and growing more so all the time.

But it's all the same to her. She doesn't think in terms of leagues and wouldn't care if she did, for which he's tremendously grateful. And she has never understood why their being a couple is a head-scratcher to many. Like the downtown hotel chef manning the prime rib station at the extremely gala fundraiser they attended who asked, after he served Tamila and she moved on to get a roll, "Is *she* really married to *you*?" Or the perhaps slightly tipsy (but only slightly) gentleman who did a double take after they crossed paths on the sidewalk and called out, "Old man, you got it goin' *on!*"

So when she laughs about Jim and Julianna's "puppy love" (as she's been calling it) he is tempted (*be honest*) to describe their text exchanges, just to make her laugh harder. But the careful man reminds him that some things really are best left unmentioned.

On Saturday morning, having confirmed his wife's safe arrival in Morant Bay, Jim turns determinedly to his work; he's been planning to use the solitary hours to catch up on an enormous backlog. But he has difficulty concentrating. Knowing he will be without Tamila for almost a month (much longer than they've ever been apart since they first met) is spookily reminiscent of being alone in the two-bedroom apartment he and Patricia shared with Peter the dog walker when he was twenty-five, after Patricia walked out on him and Peter got very sick and had to go to his parents' home in Clearwater to recuperate. It's still hard to accept what a wounded, half-blind mess he was at that age, while grasping how much saner and healthier he's become in AT (*anno Tamila*) 27 can be even harder. But what he persistently experiences as he wanders the house trying to find the book he put down or carefully washes up after making himself eggs over easy yet again reminds him sharply of that bereft, confusional time. "You'd think work would be an antidote," he says to King Kong (Tami has a kitsch fetish) after restoring his toothbrush to the ape's encircling arm. But so far no.

Still he has to keep trying. So Wednesday evening, five days into living alone, he is at it again, on the sofa this time in hopes that getting away from his fucking "home office" in a corner of the guest room will make things easier. And it does seem to, a little. He might manage to cross off a list item tomorrow.

But suddenly someone is knocking so despite his modest progress he gladly puts aside the hated computer, jumps up, buttons his shirt, and turns on the hall light as he goes to open the door, wondering with an odd little thrill who could be outside it at nine-thirty on a rainy August evening.

It's Julianna. Julie. In a blue slicker like a kid's, with the hood hanging over her forehead so her eyes shine as if from a cave. He can't even see her mouth, really, just her eyes. He is beginning to be alarmed by how long they've stood silently peering at each other when she says (without blinking) "Do you want to fuck me?"

His first impulse, close on the heels of reflexive delight and *holy crap!*, is to hedge in some way, like he's not sure he understands. *Be honest*, he reminds himself.

"Is that a query or a proposition?"

"The former."

"Well, yes. Of course I do."

"Now it's the latter."

Then they're back to the peering, but after a couple of seconds it becomes intolerable so he steps aside and gestures her into the house. In the hallway she turns her back on him, confusing him terribly until he realizes she wants him to help her off with her slicker, which will almost certainly involve touching her. After a moment's further pause he gives it a try and indeed it does, although the contact is only glancing. Without a word she walks into the living room. As he hangs her slicker on the rack, taking care that it's over the boot tray to catch the dripping, he clarifies to himself very explicitly that he is *alone in the house with Julianna* and will remain so until one of them leaves.

When he joins her she's already sitting in the armchair nearest the end of the sofa where he was working. Her hands are folded in her lap. Her bright yellow summer dress, its skirt wet in spots, is typical of her—just a bit revealing and very feminine, which together with her, well, classic shape makes it quite appealing— and her leather sandals are soaked. He should offer her slippers. And a bathrobe. He sits in the middle of the sofa rather than at the end but still feels ridiculously close.

"I never imagined you would consider such a thing."

"Neither did I."

Another intolerable, locked-eyes silence.

"Look, Julianna—"

"Julie. I insist."

"I'll call you Julie if you'll stop with the sphinx business and admit you've driven this well past the edge of harmless without my consent."

"Call me what you want. I'm much more interested in whether you're going to fuck me."

"Honestly, Julie!"

"As to obtaining your consent, Jimmy Jenks, beyond the absurdity of a man insisting on such a thing, your response to my query was unequivocal."

"Concerning whether I want to. Not whether I will."

"So you're saying no? Really? After seven years of your tongue hanging out so far I'm amazed Tamila hasn't cut it off for you?"

"I've confessed to my desire and as you say you've been aware of it for a while, so let's consider it stipulated. And I haven't said no."

"You haven't said yes, either. And speaking of driving things off the edge, when an attractive woman declares her interest you can hesitate only so long before she begins to think better of it."

He is absolutely, completely out of his depth. Could anything have prepared him for this?

"Excuse me, a *sparklingly* attractive woman."

What a nightmare. That he absolutely got himself into. Not an apt term, generally speaking, for the perfect opportunity for extramarital adventure with a longtime object of desire. But in this case, for this man, it seems to fit.

"Would you like some slippers? Those wet sandals must be unpleasant."

"Honestly, Jimmy!"

"I'm sorry?"

"Yes I want to take them off. No I do not want slippers. Nor do I want a robe to replace my dress when I remove it. I want to warm up under the covers with you. I've made that clear, haven't I?"

"I can't—"

"You *can't*? Do you know, James, that in my total of twenty-five or so years with two different partners, despite the large number of men—sorry, I hate to sound vain, but we really are talking about a pretty large number—I could have tried this with who would definitely be under those covers with me by this point, I haven't once? And now the honor is yours and you *can't*? Do you understand what happens when someone finally takes the plunge and finds no water in the pool?"

"Julie. I'm sorry. I do want to. But I can't." *Be honest.* "No, I won't. I'm too old for that kind of trouble."

"They'll never know. And surely you realize Julianna won't cause a fuss."

"We'll—"

"*Please* don't say 'we'll know'. That's the whole point."

"The trouble would be with myself."

"Jimmy, you suggested I be Julie. Okay, here she is. I just want a couple of hours with her before going back to that depressive, inhibited, condescending bitch. My god, am I asking so much?"

He has no idea how long it's been since he was in tears with anyone but Tamila. A long, long time. He thought he would never have to do anything like this again.

"Oh Jim," she says, resting her arms on the chair and straightening a little, as if posing. She is lovely. "*You* have nothing to be wretched about."

For whatever reason—because it's honest, maybe?—this calms him a little. She waits a long moment for his reply and then sighs.

"I'm going to take the sandals off, okay? I'll leave the dress for now so you won't panic."

Watching her graceful movements, her elegant limbs, he's astonished all over again by the impression she naturally conveys. It occurs to him that her (there is no other word for it) freakishly fresh appearance could be supernaturally linked to the "bitch" she referred to, some Dorian Gray type of bargain in which her soul is degraded by joyless self-affliction while her body remains unworn and untorn.

She tosses the sandals aside, sets both feet flat on the floor and leans forward as if readying herself to stand. "I know you all wonder why I'm with Bish. Why we're not married, just how committed we are, blah blah." She draws a deep but uneven breath. "You know how everyone goes on about how the pandemic has *changed* things? For me it's been more of the same. A lot more. During the fourteen months of being confined to quarters—and it really was that, you know how scared he's been—I might have been reassessing the question, don't you think? Any normal person would." She hesitates. "But I'm not normal, Jim."

"No?"

"I spent that time, it seemed like every bloody second, reviewing the reasons Bish has not to be with *me* ..."

He is momentarily almost amused because she looks for all the world as if she's just said something surprising, even shocking. As if he never heard anything so weak and pathetic and will now want her out of his sight.

"We all have thoughts of that kind sometimes. And I think an awful lot of people must have had them even more this past year. It stands to reason."

She briskly shakes her head. "'Thoughts of that kind' are what I always think. And have every day since I can remember. Being stuck in that house trying to look after each other just made it clearer than ever that nothing about Bish even matters. No one else's flaws or virtues have *ever* mattered, given it's impossible for anyone to benefit from my existence."

"Are you serious? Bish adores you."

"Maybe he does. How does that make him better off?"

"Julie. As I said, most people feel that way at times. With or without the virus."

She is suddenly angry, her entire body quivering. *"Haven't you been listening?* I said *all* the time. As in I'm never *not* doing it. What part of *depressive inhibited bitch* do you not understand? I'm trying to fucking tell you that I've never looked in the mirror and seen anything worth saving! That there's a switch on my butt with two positions, self-*doubt* and self-*hatred*, I'm an anti-Julianna *machine* …" And now she is the one in tears.

All at once he can see it: they share nothing to be proud of and everything to be pitied. He's been luckier, that's all.

"Julie. Listen. This is awful. I'm so sorry."

She sits weeping, one hand covering her mouth and the other clutching the armrest, staring into space.

"I didn't get it at first, but I'm starting to. It's painful. I'd like to help."

"Would you?" she whispers, turning her face down and away. He does hurt for her, a lot; it's like seeing a photo of a smashed-up car with his own corpse inside.

"I would. But not what you asked for."

"You want to."

"Yes. But it wouldn't do you any good. My god, Julie, I'm not important. *Wanting*'s not important. Needing is. What do you need? That made you come here?"

After a long pause she looks up; they lock eyes as they did at the door, a million years ago. "A friend, apparently."

He sighs as she tries to sustain contact but then lowers her head again, like a dog about to be scolded. Or whipped. She really believes she invented all this misery.

"I've been trying to be your friend for a long time, actually. You certainly haven't made it easy—or rather Julianna hasn't—but you know I've been trying. Yes you look good to me but I want to fuck you because I *like* you. A lot. Or at least hope to. And would have long since except it's so goddamn hard to get close to you."

He sounds exactly like Patricia telling him the very same thing, a very long time ago.

After what must be at least a minute—*be patient*, he tells himself, *when it's the honest thing to do*—she says, "I'd like to revise my query, James. If I may."

"Please."

"Do you want to be my friend?"

"I really do. Even more than I thought."

"And as a proposition?"

"Agreed."

More silence. More patience.

"So we'll go on a date."

"I'm sorry?"

"While they're away. To get to know each other better. So you can be sure you actually like me instead of just hoping."

"But we won't ..."

She sighs, looks up at last, rolls her eyes. "We won't go there, okay? Although we *could*."

"We surely could." At that it's hard, for a moment, to let it go.

"So what do you say?"

"You're on, Julie. It'll be fun."

She raises her head all the way and sits up straight, looking a lot better, and he knows he is grinning. The nightmare may soon be over. And he's earned his peace for once.

"There's one more thing, though, Jimmy."

"Oh?"

"I need to touch you."

"Oh?"

"It won't be real otherwise."

Their eyes are locked again; *be honest*, hers say.

"I guess that's true."

"I'm going to come and sit on your lap."

He manages a nod.

"Don't be frightened."

"I'm not."

She opens her mouth, thinks better of it, stands up, walks to the sofa, and gently lowers and rearranges herself until she is in his lap, her legs folded across his, leaning against him. His hands are by his sides, on the upholstery.

"Only hold me."

Be brave, he thinks. *Be open. For a little while be kind without worrying what it might cost you.* So he takes her in his arms and devotes himself to holding her as tenderly and affectionately as he can, given his ignorance of her heart. Which he swears he can feel beating.

After a long passage of time he has no means of measuring she says, "This is very nice, Jimmy Jenks."

"It is very nice, Julie Jules."

She sighs and touches her forehead to his. Her eyes are very close.

"Is it enough?" he asks. "Along with knowing how much I really would like to fuck you? How I'm resisting with all my strength because I'm mortally certain that's not what you want for either of us, to be people who would do that sort of thing?"

She closes her eyes. For a man recently in turmoil he is astonishingly content. Just holding her. Like it's something he's needed forever—not since their first meeting, not since he was thirteen and aching to take a girl's hand, but forever. And even more astonishing is that he will be equally content to stop, in a little while, and never do it anymore.

When she opens them again her eyes are somehow even closer, although neither of them has moved. When she answers him it's a whisper.

"I think," she tells him, "that it might. Might be enough. If you also kiss me. If you kiss me I think I might really, truly know what you really, truly want. And that would be enough." She raises her head and he can see, with greater distance, how much it matters.

He smiles. "I'm willing to try," he tells her, taking her face in his hands.

She smiles back, a dazzling smile; on Julianna it's a virtual sunburst. He is sure she has never come close. She *is* a different person, at least for this moment. It won't last, but she'll remember.

"To my sparkling side," she says, leaning in.

The Uses of Time

Daniel was definitely late, if not yet terribly so. Although Carly had recently become more tolerant of small faults, tardiness could still rile her. So as an exercise in forbearance she committed herself to not being stressed by or even caring how late he was, and glancing at her watch decided she would graciously allow him another quarter hour before calmly leaving. After all he had her number if something was holding him up. And if he'd simply decided against coming at all she had plenty of work to get back to, the sooner the better.

Not that she wasn't enjoying the break from the office, to which she remained a semi-stranger, and the expansive experience of sitting in the plaza for the first time in nearly two years on a lovely late summer day. The scene looked almost back to normal; it was once again a festive space, and while the air of privilege that had always hung over it like a slap in the face was still a bit attenuated by the viral scourges of apprehension, hesitation and uncertainty, it was clearly returning in strength.

Looking over the familiar young tech worker crowd she was disappointed but not surprised to find herself as irked by their sensibility, their apparently indiscriminate acceptance of their blessings, as she'd been in the Before Time. She expected it from her affluent agemates but these kids knew better. Probably eight

201

in ten had condemned white supremacy, demanded queer rights, supported their school district's striking maintenance workers before their sixteenth birthdays, yet here they sat looking for all the world as if this was the way everyone lived.

And in case that wasn't enough, by lifting her gaze she could see the upper floors of the building near hers — the one where Lexi and both Joshes worked — that had recently sold for an absurd price per square foot, some kind of record apparently. On learning this she'd quickly calculated that her cozy window office with its stunning view of the basin, the bridge and the statehouse would at the quoted figure be worth as much as Robert and Ricardo had paid for the charming Pioneer Valley four-bedroom they'd just escaped to. Absurd but equally unsurprising. She lived in a territory whose inhabitants happily accepted their estrangement from their own flesh and blood, even if they didn't know it.

And here *she* sat all the same, among the entitled, drinking a dollar's worth of gin, tonic and lime juice that would cost her nine. Maybe she knew better but it was where she belonged. Just as she'd soon return to her "cozy" office, big enough to house a family in many countries, and enjoy the impressive panorama of buildings far enough away to make the suffering in which they were rooted invisible. It was true she'd managed to stop griping aloud but griping to herself still made her a hypocrite. She too accepted her luck without complaint.

As it turned out Daniel arrived with only minutes to spare. She'd been passing the time reviewing the crowd and as she examined one young woman in a fetching and very short magenta sundress who looked from a distance, as she stood by a high table outside the Blue Room talking to two very attentive young men, to be as strikingly perfect in appearance as Miriam Espinosa had been in their senior year of high school, Carly saw him walk briskly around the corner and stop abruptly at the edge of the patio, peering this way and that like some burrowing animal up for air. She was thinking about waving when he found and started toward her.

She *was* nervous, a little. As he came she had a peculiar sense that something was off, misaligned or out of scale, but she chalked it up to the time passed and his unkempt haircut and smiled as he approached. His face was still handsome and kind, at any rate.

"It's so nice to see you after so long, Daniel."

"Yeah. A year and a half. Don't get up."

At least he looked away as he said it. Honestly she wanted to stand, grab her bag, and march the fuck out of there. She'd lived too long not to be shut of people immature or self-centered enough to let sarcasm be the first thing out of their mouth on an occasion like this. But she was halfway through her drink and had no cash to fling on the table.

"This isn't going to be friendly, I take it."

"Sorry," he said. "I'm really very sorry, Carly. I'm very happy to see you too."

"Why don't you sit down?"

He obediently sat but there were no further comments, sarcastic or otherwise, and precious little eye contact. It came to her that the out of sync thing was at least in part the absence of the striped button-down shirt and gray dress slacks she'd always seen him in. Clearly his new firm had the normal industry standards for engineering decorum.

"How are you?" she asked.

"I'm well, generally. I hope you are too?" She nodded. He clearly *was* sorry, not that he shouldn't be. "I'm glad. I'm so glad to know it." Glancing at her tall glass, he asked, "Is that a drink? With liquor I mean? Because truthfully how I am right now is in need of one."

Spotting her server coming more or less their way, she Anne Bancrofted him over. As he arrived he asked "What would you like, sir?" and for a fleeting, Hoffmanesque moment Daniel seemed very much as though what he'd like most of all was not to be sitting with Carly. But he got a grip and managed "High-rye whisky, if you have it."

"Redemption?"

"Absolutely. On the rocks please."

He watched the waiter walk away for a second too long and took a sharp breath as he turned to her. But he was sticking with small talk for the moment.

"How's the old shop?"

"Same as all the others, I guess—trying to refocus. We've been having quite a fuss about 'return to office' because Sandy and Pauline were fairly clueless at first about how much things have changed. But I think it's calming down now."

"How are Miranda and the group doing?"

She laughed. "I'm a little out of touch—none of her projects are in my new portfolio—but I think your departure must still have them struggling." No laugh from him but at least he smiled. Finally.

"Miranda was the best dev manager I ever worked for."

She wondered if a four-year career could legitimately support the word *ever*. "Along with being the most attractive coder in town?"

He looked embarrassed, then laughed. Which was nice to hear.

"Foolish of me, wasn't it?"

"You meant it in a respectful way."

"I was fairly sure you wouldn't report me."

"I don't think it qualifies as harassment if she never knew it happened."

And there the conversation died, or at least fell into gentle slumber. Neither seemed interested in continuing. *If we were honest,* she thought, *we would get up, embrace for a long minute, kiss each other's cheeks and go our separate ways forever.* But this was clearly not going to happen, so after briefly surveying the plaza again—the Miriam type was gone—she impulsively decided to force things.

"Daniel, why did you want to meet?"

"Believe me, Carly, I've tried not to bother you. I've spent pretty much every day since my second shot trying not to bother you."

"I wasn't concerned about you 'bothering' me. It would have been nice to hear from you."

"Actually," he went on, as if she hadn't used the word *nice* for the second time or even spoken at all, "I'm more or less certain that changing jobs was at bottom an effort to minimize the opportunity and temptation."

"But?"

He was staring at his hands.

"I need to know why," he told her, quietly. "I've made a very thorough run at the accepting not knowing thing and it's done me no good." He watched her face for a second or two without finding what he was searching for, apparently, then turned to his hands again. "I mean, I imagine you don't much like the thought of me obsessing over you. If I can understand what happened that can stop."

"Well I didn't know you were! So of course I didn't mind."

"I'm not blaming you for my obsession."

"But for something else?"

The server brought the whiskey and pointed at Carly's empty gin and tonic; she shook her head and he retreated.

"How about this," said Daniel, after taking a couple of sips. "Let me ask my question and then maybe, if it seems worth our while, we can start assessing blame."

She had no idea how he meant this. "Fair enough."

"Why did you lead me on?"

"Why did I *what*? Lead you *on*? Is that what you just asked me?"

"Yeah."

"It's an ugly accusation."

"You're right, and I retract it. Let me try again. How is it that a twenty-six year old who was clearly in love with you was allowed to persuade himself for so long that you were both single and not terribly far from his age when you were happily married and considerably older—old enough to be his mother, in point of fact?"

For a moment she wanted to temporize and, well, snark back at him by pointing out that a much younger woman would be old enough for that. But she gave him the answer he deserved.

"Because I was in love with you too."

Was *flabbergasted* the word? she wondered. Maybe *dumbfounded*? If she were to someday qualify his expression to a friend, which she was never, ever going to do, she would probably say *stupefied*, a word she had actually been known to use.

She gave him time to respond but he was more or less frozen. "I didn't know it," she went on. "I mean I didn't know I knew it. I *prevented* myself from knowing. Which even without some particular personal circumstances I'm prepared to describe if you want I think you'll acknowledge I had plenty of reasons to do. Foremost among them that I was enjoying it so much."

Could you cry while stupefied? Obviously yes. Equally obvious was that having just stupefied someone to tears you could be quite tempted to join in, while at the same time well aware of the drawbacks of sitting among the carefree lunchtime crowd in your expensive tailored suit weeping with a guy wearing very worn jeans and a HackMIT t-shirt.

"You also had plenty of reasons to just tell me who you were. If I meant so much to you."

"In point of a couple of facts, Daniel, while I'm glad you think I'm youthful I'm quite sure I look more or less my age, and I was *always* wearing my wedding ring. This one here? I wasn't hiding anything."

"You were. You never mentioned your husband to me, Carly, not once. Until that stupid lunch."

"I guess that's true."

"Where let alone *mentioning* him, you punched me in the gut in front of everyone by going on in great detail about him, about your kids—including your son almost *my exact age*—and your adorable house in your delightful neighborhood and so on. Rubbing my face in your so happy life that obviously had zero room for me."

Well I deserve this, she thought. She'd been reliving that scene, suffering over it, for a year and a half, and his recap was like an assault.

"Daniel. Can we take a step back here and recall that for all that may have been going on under the surface we were simply work friends? By level of acquaintance?"

"*May* have been?"

It was her turn to look at her hands.

"Carly. I don't know what you mean by 'under the surface' but I know what I saw when you smiled. I know what I heard when you greeted me at the bike stand. I know what I read in our chats, all those nice things you said, those *intimate* things. The nicknames. So please don't come at me with *work friends*. Please."

She was concerned that stupefied would soon be overtaken by combative and felt an urgent pang. *Just tell him.* "For all the time you've been remembering all of this," she said, "and comforting yourself by labeling me callous and dismissive, I've been remembering too. And thinking of you. Talking to you. I've explained so many times I could do it in my sleep. So if you can set aside your wounded outrage long enough to listen—I'm sorry, I didn't mean that, I'm really *not* dismissive—I can maybe answer your question."

Why on earth had she refused that second drink?

Among the things that had drawn her to him were his emotional intelligence and remarkable, almost inviolable openness, and she could actually follow the process of his growing inclination to believe her. Although still a little teary he was definitely less angry, and more willing to listen. Which somehow made her highly aware of the part of her—just a small part, but a lively one—that was willing to run away.

Daniel closed his eyes and nodded.

"Please give me a minute. Or three."

"Of course."

But all these pauses were rough on her, Carly was realizing, gave her too much time to consider the angles, and as she sat there watching this young man she'd once cared so much for sit four feet that might as well have been a million miles away, feeling god knows what behind his silence and closed eyes, it struck her that maybe she couldn't deliver on what she'd promised. She definitely, without question wanted him to know all about it; why else would she have told him dozens, probably hundreds of times? But now that rehearsals were over and her cue was coming up, those lines she could say in her sleep—the ones about being so terrified of rejection and abandonment as a girl and young woman that she pushed away anyone who even looked like they might get close and thus had absolutely no experience of intimate relationships until the age of twenty-nine—suddenly seemed far less plausible. At least for an audience who'd once been a fan but now might sit on his hands. And while admitting to herself after months of shame and depression that she *couldn't* have recognized that she was falling in love because she'd never done it before— that she'd been a highly educated, sophisticated woman wholly unaware of her parallel existence as a breathless adolescent waiting for real life to begin—had been painful, grievously painful, sobbing quietly in the kitchen at midnight hoping your husband won't wake up and hear painful, this might be less than convincing to Daniel. Who actually *was* young, who couldn't have her any more than she could have him but had no alternative to fall back on.

Of course she badly wanted to clarify that the gut punch (she'd used exactly that term to her therapist, to the houseplants, to the dog as they kept their social and every other kind of distance from the legion of brave solitary women and dogs around them on their endless futile walks) had really been aimed at herself and she was sorry he was struck by it too, but this might be the least defensible claim of all; as stated, pushing away was what she knew. The whole drama hadn't made a bit of sense to her until she'd beaten it to death over a long period of time and expecting him to encompass it all at once, to do anything but laugh or curse suddenly looked unrealistic. In fact it seemed to her more and more as the minutes went by that "It was wonderful knowing you, it was a gift to fall in love with you, I'm so sorry about the pain, goodbye" might well be a better approach.

But she'd promised. And what was the point of all those months spent coming to grips with it—trying not to break down every time she thought of him, cursing herself for that punch despite the utter certainty that having him close was not only knowingly faithless but a serious risk and always would be, making it a burden he would eventually come to despise—if she didn't share now? He *had* in fact given her a gift, a profound one she'd never dreamed she might receive, didn't know she was in need of. So at least she could try.

It came to her as she waited: pushing and pulling were mostly the same. Then his eyes finally opened and she was startled by the change in them.

"You know what? You're off the hook," he said, almost calmly.

"Off the hook?"

"I don't need to know."

"But I'm happy to—"

"I don't actually *want* to know, Carly."

It was really very unlikely that anyone from her office would be coming through the plaza on this particular day. And who the fuck had reason to care if they did and encountered her in tears across a stupid patio table from HackMIT? Although she suspected tomorrow might be different, there and then giving vent to pent-up despair seemed not only appropriate but a treat. There had been plenty for the past year and there was plenty ahead and what with her fifty-year backlog she'd better start cranking up the throughput if she was going to process it all by her so-called golden years. If they ever arrived.

Daniel watched her cry for a while. Then he sighed, got up and came to her, waited for her to stand, put his arms around her and held while her heart flew to her mouth and back again, kissed her wet cheek, said "I'm so glad to have known you, Carly. I'm sorry

it's hard but for me it was worth it. For you too I hope. Goodbye."
At the last word of which she closed her eyes tight, tighter than he
had, much tighter, because while she was required to accept this,
to content herself with never telling him, never saying the truth to
anyone ever, she was absolutely not going to watch him walk
away, this time for good; that at least she was permitted, entitled,
privileged to avoid if she wished. Which she very much did. And
when she was willing to look again, which was not for some time,
a time sufficient for all her regrets, all, to come flooding back to
drown her, he was entirely lost from sight.

If you're glad you read this book, there are a couple of favors I hope you'll consider doing me:

o Pass it on to someone else! (Then I'll owe you, like, a hundred favors.)

o Rate it on Amazon. (That's for all the people you can't recommend it to personally.)

o Follow me on Twitter @rcbinstock.

o Go to my website, rcbinstock.com, and check out my other books.

o Write me at rcbinstockbooks@gmail.com, I'd love to hear from you.

Every reader is a treasure, and every page read a gift. Thank you!

— R.C. Binstock

R.C. Binstock lives in Cambridge, Massachusetts. At Harvard College he studied writing with Ann Beattie, Monroe Engel, and Grace Mojtabai. *What You Can't Give Me* is his second book of stories. His first collection, *The Light of Home*, was published in 1992 (Atheneum), followed by his novels *Tree of Heaven* in 1995 and *The Soldier* in 1996 (Soho Press). He has self-published four novels: *Swift River* (2014), an author's edition of *Tree of Heaven* (2015), *Native Child* (2016), and *The Vanished* (2018).

Follow R.C. Binstock on Twitter @rcbinstock, and find him on the web at http://rcbinstock.com.

Printed in Great Britain
by Amazon

86320607R00132